RESIST

Among Us Trilogy book 2

ANNE-RAE VASQUEZ

Developmental editor
JOSEFINA ROSADO

Augmented Reality
PUBLISHING

CONTENTS

This is a work of fiction. The events and characters described here are purely fictional and in no way represent or resemble real life events, places or people.

a Truth Seekers end of the world religious thriller series

Among Us Trilogy. Copyright © 2013 by AR Publishing, Anne-Rae Vasquez

www.amongus.ca www.anne-raevasquez.com

Developmental Editor: Josefina Rosado

Editor: Dayne Edmondson

Cover graphic design by Vanesa Garkova

ISBN 978-0992145842 AR Publishing

Amazon Print 2nd edition

✵ Created with Vellum

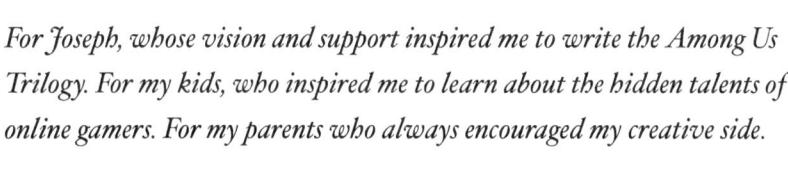

For Joseph, whose vision and support inspired me to write the Among Us Trilogy. For my kids, who inspired me to learn about the hidden talents of online gamers. For my parents who always encouraged my creative side.

For Josefina, who pushed the borders of my creativity to help me bring Harry, Kerim, and Cristal to life.

Finally, for you, my Truth Seekers who dared to believe.

NOTE FROM PUBLISHER

If you haven't read *Doubt book 1 of the Among Us Trilogy*, we highly recommend you do so before continuing. But if you want to move forward, we've provided you with a plot summary and a list of Characters at the end of the book.

Sign up to become a member of the Truth Seekers book club!

PROLOGUE

The sixty-foot-high walls of Akko now sat in a pile of dust on the beach. Harry stared at Cristal as white pillars of light shot from the ground, through her body, into the reddened sky. If you asked him twenty-four hours ago if he'd believe this could happen, he would have calmly said, "scientifically speaking, yes." But standing and witnessing supernatural events before his eyes, all his confidence in reality was now shot to pieces.

Cristal appeared calm as she watched the video playing on his phone, oblivious to the fact that she was radiating energy like a nuclear explosion. Gabriel had captured the video on his phone before he was killed trying to save Kerim. It was the same video that revealed Kerim's true mission - "Destroy Cristal to save the spiritual world." Who knew that Kerim was a covert guardian angel? The words sounded hilarious in his head, even after witnessing it with his own eyes.

After a few minutes, Cristal pushed Harry's phone away from her.

"Harry, this is too much. I'm part of a bloodline that has special powers?"

Harry followed Cristal's gaze and saw Raffe and Kerim arguing with each other. The ground was shaking and buildings were collapsing around them.

"Harry, I'm going to try to close the portal," Cristal said.

"Wait! I have to go through it," he said, grabbing her shoulders. "I believe my mother and your father are there on the other side, in Limbo or whatever Raffe and Kerim were talking about." He looked at her with determination in his eyes.

"Yes, they have been trying to communicate with us. I think they are alive. I **know** they are alive."

"I will do my best to bring them back," he said, touching her face.

"I know you will, Harry," she said. She looked defiant, no longer afraid or in denial of her abilities.

"Hurry, before they see you," she said. "I'll close the portal after you enter. I will make sure Raffe and Kerim don't follow you."

The look of concern in her eyes made him want to stay. Protect her. But really, what kind of protector could he be to her? She was the one with special powers.

Harry leaned in close to speak in her ear. "Take care of yourself, okay?" he said.

"Yeah, you know I always do."

She smirked and looked into his eyes.

"Hurry up before I zap you with my super-duper energy blast."

He smiled. It was just like old times.

"I'll be back soon," he said. The thunder roared around them.

He wasn't sure what was on the other side but he knew he had to take the chance. He stepped into the light and crossed to the other side.

PART I
CROSSING WORLDS

a bird in a cage holding a broken wing
staring through bars of lies and deceit
as she perches on a broken swing
while the rope that cuts the claw
opens wounds to bleed

AR Vasquez

CHAPTER 1
BETWEEN LIFE AND DEATH

H arry stepped through the light, his foot landing on thin air. He keeled forward expecting to hit the ground head-first but instead he was suspended in a void of emptiness—a dark vacuum.

"Anyone out there?" he asked.

He was met with dead silence. Funny he should think that. Was this what being dead felt like?

Enough. Focus on the mission.

He had to find his mother and Cristal's father and bring them back to the land of the living.

"Mom, can you hear me?" he called out.

Nothing but silence met his query. He began to wonder if he had made the right decision to cross over to the spiritual world. What if crossing over meant he had to die doing it?

A sharp pain stabbed his heart. He grabbed his chest until the pain subsided to a dull ache. He was somewhat relieved that he still had a beating heart. It proved he wasn't dead after all.

Maybe time stood still on this side. What if he ended up floating here in spiritual emptiness forever?

"Harry?" his mother's voice entered the void.

"Mom?" he called out. "Mom!"

Twisting his body, he tried to float towards the sound.

Something icy grabbed his arm and yanked him downward. He began free falling into the abysmal blackness.

Should he brace himself for the landing?

Before another thought could enter his mind, his body slammed into a solid surface, knocking him out on impact.

⚜

WHAT SEEMED LIKE HOURS LATER, BUT COULD HAVE BEEN minutes, he gained consciousness, realizing that he was laying flat on his back. Sounds and voices of people around him and the honking of car horns jolted him awake.

"Harry!"

The voice sounded so familiar and yet he couldn't place it. His eyes were trying to adjust to the bright light.

"Thank God! It is you, Harry."

Harry felt someone pull himself into a sitting position.

"Are you okay?"

He glanced up to see who the Good Samaritan was, but instead he was staring dumbfounded at the lopsided grin of someone he didn't expect to ever see again.

"Harry! I'm so glad I found you! I thought I was going crazy!"

"Gabriel?"

"I don't know what happened. I was rushing towards you and Kerim and then you all disappeared."

Harry racked his brain to comprehend what was happening.

8

He, along with Cristal and the others, had watched Gabriel get shot in the back and die in the street. But here was Gabriel in the flesh right in front of him. He reached out to touch Gabriel's arm, half expecting to feel nothingness. Surely, he must be hallucinating.

"I've been trying to find the others but nobody here has seen them," Gabriel said. "Here, let me help you up."

Gabriel grabbed hold of Harry's arm and put it over his shoulder, easing him up to his feet.

Harry took a deep breath. The salty sea air mixed with the smell of diesel smoke spewing from the tailpipes of cars driving by filled his lungs.

Wait a minute. Where am I?

He scanned his surroundings.

It was incredible. They were standing in the same spot where Yaffa and her security thugs had shot Gabriel down.

He glanced around, feeling disoriented. The sun was setting against the turquoise blue sky. The streets were busy with young men smoking *sheesha* water pipes, laughing and horsing around on the beach. This was not what Harry had expected to see in Limbo or Purgatory or whatever this place was.

"Harry, you look like you've seen a ghost," Gabriel said.

Harry swallowed hard and forced a smile.

Doesn't he remember being killed?

Harry's Truth Seeker skills kicked in. He didn't know what would happen if he told Gabriel the cold hard facts. Better to go along with the situation until he could figure out what was happening.

"I'm not feeling well. Why don't we go find a place to talk?" Harry asked.

"Sure thing. We can get you something to eat."

Harry let Gabriel walk ahead while he scanned landmarks around him, making note of the location of where the portal would have been on the "other side". It was the place where the walls of Akko used to stand before they crumbled into dust during the earthquake. Here on this side of reality a wall of steel bars stood between the street and the sea.

If I'm going to get back to the other side, I have to come back to this spot.

"Harry, c'mon. The others will be relieved to see you."

Others?

"Uh, Gabriel. What others?" Harry asked, but Gabriel had darted ahead.

He followed Gabriel into the small shop. It was a typical fast food restaurant in the area. Sharp smells of spices and greasy food hit his nostrils while the sound of Arabic pop music blasted from a boom box sitting on a shelf behind the front counter. Groups of young people sat at the wooden tables spread across the room. A number of the guys glanced up, eyeing him suspiciously as he walked past.

Gabriel waved to someone sitting at a table in the back of the shop.

"Look who I've found!"

As he walked closer, Harry could see two people sitting across from each other at the table. One was a woman with her back to him and the other was a middle-aged man with Latino features, olive complexion, dark wavy hair, and a pointed nose.

When they reached the table, the woman stood up and turned to face him. Harry's heart started racing when their eyes met.

"Mom?"

It had been a long time since he last saw his mother Bina. She was thinner; her hair was greyer and the wrinkles around her eyes deeper than he remembered.

Waves of emotion ran through him. Every cell in his body wanted to run to her and hug her just as he did when he was a terrified six-year-old child lost in a crowded shopping mall.

The look of concern on her face and the way she glanced over her shoulder forced him to realize that this was not the time or the place. The reunion celebration would have to wait until their safety was established.

"Harry, we need to be discreet," she said in a hushed voice. "Sit down beside me and face Roberto."

She motioned with her hand towards the man sitting across from her. Roberto lifted his chin slightly in acknowledgement.

Gabriel asked, "So you know Rose?"

Harry shot a glance at his mother. Was *Rose* her alias?

Harry's mother turned to Gabriel.

"Please keep your voice down and take a seat."

Gabriel took the chair beside Roberto while Harry sat down beside her. There were many questions he wanted to ask but he remained quiet. The answers would come, all in good time.

The loud music and the noise from the different conversations in the room decreased in volume. Harry checked over his shoulder to see that all eyes were on them.

Roberto lowered his voice, speaking with a subtle Spanish accent, "Harry, your mother Bina has taken the alias Rose and you must refer to her as this until we get out of here."

Gabriel's eyebrows shot up and his mouth opened as if to say something.

Harry pulled his focus back to Roberto.

"I'm assuming that Roberto is not your real name either," Harry said.

"Correct. I'm Carlos Hernandez. Cristal's father."

CHAPTER 2
NOW WHAT?

It took some time to process what Cristal's dad was saying. Harry sat trying his best to be patient as Carlos aka Roberto rambled on in what seemed to be coded words.

"Rose and I have been trying to contact you and Mist for some time now."

Gabriel smiled and whispered, "I told them what Cristal's alias was."

Harry narrowed his eyes. Unlike Gabriel, he still didn't fully trust this person sitting across from him. Carlos could have been involved in the kidnapping of his mother. Under the circumstances, he wasn't about to trust anyone blindly.

Carlos continued. "Every time we were able to send a message to either of you, the military would show up. We had to keep running. But we stopped here in Akko, where Rose felt the strongest connection with both of you."

Carlos placed his elbows on the table and leaned towards Harry.

"Is Mist safe? Did she survive the ..." Carlos glanced at Gabriel for a half-second before turning back to Harry and said, "...the event? Did she survive the event?"

Gabriel's face clouded over in confusion but he remained quiet, staring at Harry in hopes that his answer would clarify things.

Harry looked straight into Carlos's dark eyes.

"Yes, Mist is safe. She survived the event."

Carlos drew a deep sigh and sat back.

"Good. The air raid sirens went off a few hours ago. The military surrounded the area outside this shop," Carlos said. "Rose and I had been able to successfully send messages from here through to you and Mist. In Rose's vision, she saw a blinding white light erupting from the ground near the gates outside. It shot up to the sky and through the light she was able to see everything on your side."

Harry's mother turned towards him. He noticed her body trembling just a little, her dark brown eyes searching his as she spoke.

"What I saw was similar to a dream I had," she said.

"You mean the one you wrote in your journal?"

He had read and reread all the entries his mother had written in hopes it would help solve the mystery of her disappearance.

"Mom," he began. "I mean, Rose. Can we find a safer place to talk, just you and me? I don't like how everyone in the restaurant is eyeing us."

His mother shot a glance at Carlos, who nodded his head as if giving her permission to speak.

"Harry," she said. "Roberto and I are, let's say, joined together."

Gabriel asked, "Joined together? As in marriage?"

Harry raised an eyebrow. *Keep calm. Just listen.*

Carlos interrupted. "No, no, no. She means joined together by an invisible force. We cannot move more than twenty-feet away from each other."

Harry's eyebrow arched higher as he turned to his mother.

"Did they do this to you at Global Nation?" he asked.

His mother started wringing her hands together, a habit she did when she was under extreme stress.

"A few hours after I started my first day of volunteer work at Tel Aviv's GN University, two GN security guards escorted me into secret labs two levels underground for questioning. They asked me about the experiments that your father did before his death. About the "soul" and "time travel" experiments. When I refused to tell them anything, they injected me with something that put me into a coma. I knew I was in a coma because as I lay in a comatose state, I was able to sit up and leave my body."

She stopped for a moment, her gaze switching briefly to Carlos who gave her a small smile of encouragement. She turned back to Harry and continued.

"I had left my body and started walking the halls of the underground labs. I found others being questioned and experimented on like lab animals. I wanted to escape—to run out of the building but a magnetic energy pulled me back. It kept pulling me and pulling until I reached a locked room. I looked in through the small glass window and saw a man lying on a bed, hooked up to machines. I noticed a movement on the other side of the door. It startled me so I stepped backwards to find that the man who had been in the bed was now walking through the closed door. This is how I met ..."

She fell silent, her eyes meeting Carlos' gaze.

CHAPTER 3
MEGIDDO SAFE HOUSE

It was twelve hours since she last saw Harry, Kerim and Gabriel. She had ridden away on the back of Kerim's motorcycle with Walid while Kerim flew off to who knew where.

The ride from Akko to Walid's home in Megiddo was an adventure in itself. The earthquake had lifted up the highway and tore open the asphalt. Fortunately Walid proved adept at maneuvering around the highway's cracks and crevices. She had just met him a few hours earlier but her life was now in his hands. At least until he got her to a safe place.

Compared to the scenery from the highway and the other cities where plumes of smoke rose towards the heavens and the skyline was marked with collapsed buildings, Walid's home was untouched by the earthquake. In fact the whole village seemed to have been unaffected by the event.

Walid's family welcomed her with open arms. His mother, a short chubby woman had the same warm eyes and wide smile as her son. She didn't speak a word of English but after only a few minutes Cristal was able to understand Arabic fluently.

Funny though, when Cristal tried to speak, she stumbled on the words and was unable to communicate fluently in Arabic. This hidden talent was one of many she needed to learn how to use and control.

She was given a bed to share in the room with Walid's three younger sisters who happily told her their ages and what American musicians they liked.

"Do you know JT and JayZ?" Nosayba, the youngest and the most boisterous of the three asked.

"I'm not sure who that is," she said in broken Arabic.

"Justin Teemberlake!" Nazreen, the middle one with the shy smile and shiny green eyes, exclaimed. She covered her mouth with her hand when she realized how loud she had yelled.

Shaima, the oldest girl with the long curly hair and chubby cheeks, moved in front of Cristal and said, "Please tell us how you know Justin?"

Cristal held back a giggle. She hadn't heard genuine laughter or felt such warmth in a long time. She was an only child so being around the sisters was a refreshing experience. Before she could say anything, Walid and his brother Samy entered the room. She remembered Samy from earlier on the beach when he had fetched a water bottle for her. He watched her carefully.

"Why must she stay with us, Walid?" he asked. "What if she explodes into a nuclear bomb again?"

Walid gave his younger brother a dirty look.

"Ms. Cristal is our guest and you must treat her with respect."

"Yes, *ahoo-ey*, older brother."

How could she reassure him that this wouldn't happen when she wasn't completely in control of her new found powers?

Even though she was listening intently to the conversation, her head was spinning. She tried her best to answer politely as best she could with her broken Arabic. The stress of the day had worn her down. Beads of sweat from her forehead slid down her cheek and she wiped them away with the back of her hand.

"*Immee*, Ma, bring Cristal a towel. She needs to bathe and sleep," he said.

"*Tammam*, of course. This girl has had a difficult day," his mother said.

Sometimes the things that they said didn't make much sense. Cristal realized that her brain was translating everything word for word like Google Translate, where the meanings or idioms were lost in translation.

"Come with me *bintee*, girl," Walid's mother said to her.

Cristal followed her down the hallway to a large room with three single beds. Two of the single beds were pushed together to the side of the room closest to the window. On the floor were two single futon mattresses piled on top of each other.

"You will take the bed over there."

She pointed at the single bed on the other side of the room.

Cristal wondered whose bed she was taking.

"*Im Walid*," she said in Arabic. *Im* meant Mother. Cristal pointed towards the futon mattresses on the floor. "I can sleep on the floor. The girls need to sleep in their own beds."

Walid's mother scrunched up her face in a scowl.

"*Haram*, unacceptable. No, you are the guest. Sleep in the bed," she said firmly.

Cristal nodded her head, knowing that arguing would be pointless. Walid's mother turned on her heel and walked out of the room closing the door behind her.

Cristal wondered why she had not met Walid's father. Or why

no one mentioned him. Maybe he was missing, just like her own father.

AFTER A QUICK SHOWER, SHE WENT TO BED REPLAYING ALL THE events that happened that day: Gabriel dying in her arms; the earthquake that crumbled the walls of Akko to dust; being lifted up sixty-feet in the air by a demon; being saved by Raffe, who was really an archangel, from another demon who had taken over Dr. Saeed's body; her body radiating bright white energy from the ground through her body into the sky; Harry walking through the white light to cross to the other side; and finally Kerim flying her to safety, revealing that he too was an archangel.

It was a hell of a lot to accept. The fact that she had a power within her that could open portals from the human world to the spiritual world meant she was on Heaven's top ten Most Wanted list. Why would patrons of Heaven want lowly humans and devils wandering into their exclusive country club without paying the price of membership?

She never felt so alone in her whole life. Refusing to shed a tear, the new Cristal vowed that she wasn't going to wait for someone to save her. She was going to save herself.

CHAPTER 4
LIMBO LAND

Harry was trying to piece everything together. How did his mother and Cristal's dad end up here in Limbo land? He was about to ask them just that when he sensed a commotion behind him. Carlos' eyebrow arched sharply, his gaze shifted over Harry's left shoulder. Someone or something had just entered the restaurant.

Carlos eyes darted over towards Bina. He tapped his finger on the table twice.

Harry watched his mother's body tense. She grabbed his hand under the table while the other one reached out for Gabriel's. An electric shock ran up his hand as he felt her touch. His mother's body seemed to flicker in and out—a bad hologram.

Harry looked up and saw that Gabriel and Carlos were also fading out. From the look on Gabriel's face, he was guessing, he was doing the same thing.

"Stop! I command you to stop!" a voice came from behind.

Harry could hear a loud whooshing sound behind him as he felt himself fade away.

⚜

FOR A BRIEF MOMENT HE COULD FEEL HIMSELF SUSPENDED again in nothingness before landing onto the ground. Shaken by what he could only describe as a teleportation experience, every cell in his body seemed to hum— the nerves in his fingers and toes tingling.

Gabriel stood beside him, wide-eyed and frightened.

"What just happened?" Gabriel asked him.

Harry glanced around to see that they were standing in the yard of someone's home. Two small vehicles were parked close to the five-story house. Standing by the rusty metal gates, Bina and Carlos were speaking with each other.

"Bina must have teleported us here," Harry finally managed to say.

Gabriel grabbed his arm. "Holy crap! Part of me is freaked out of my mind. The other part wants to post this on the TS forum."

Gabriel's statement should have brought their usual jovial bantering but his expression was grim, his eyes crazy with fright. Harry knew Gabriel deserved to hear the truth. But what if telling Gabriel he was dead would cause irreparable repercussions?

"Gabriel, we need to talk, but now is not the time."

Gabriel's nostrils flared and he said, "Yeah, whatever," before turning his back on him.

Harry strode over to his mother. She turned towards him and opened her arms.

"Are you going to tell us what's going on, Mom?"

Bina's arms fell to her side, the smile on her face fading.

"Yes, of course. But we'll need to talk inside. We don't know who may be listening."

Carlos stepped in between them, but moved to the side after Bina gripped his arm.

"Carlos, I can handle this. You don't need to protect me from my own son."

He took a breath and took a step back.

"Come with me," Bina said as she walked past Carlos and Gabriel. "We don't have much time."

Gabriel turned and called out, "Not much time for what?"

Carlos put his arm around Gabriel and guided him to the side of the building.

Harry could hear him say, "They need some mother and son time. We will bring you up to speed after, I promise."

Harry followed his mother up a flight of steps. When they reached the top, there was a verandah to the right and to the left a white iron gated front door. Bina waved her hand and the gate and the door opened into a narrow hallway. Light streamed from a room on the left which Harry assumed, from the fancy furniture and shiny marble tile, was a salon or a room to receive guests. Bina proceeded down the hallway where Harry picked up sounds of hushed voices coming from that direction.

"Mom, you didn't tell me that we were meeting anyone," he said in a low voice.

Bina looked up at him for a moment without missing a step. She replied, "*Far a tsap hot men moireh fun forent, far a ferd fun hinten, far a nar fun alleh zeiten.* Like I always say, every one fears a goat from in front, a horse from the rear and a fool on every side."

Harry couldn't believe it. This was just like his mother, answering him with Yiddish quotes. It was pointless asking any more questions, so he followed her, keeping his comments to himself.

The end of the hallway opened up to a large empty room. There were folding chairs arranged in rows, an indication that a meeting was about to take place. Harry could hear the voices getting louder, but he couldn't see anyone in the room.

Bina stood still, closing her eyes. She raised her hands up in the air, her palms up.

"The meeting will commence. Please take your seats everyone," she called out.

Harry wasn't sure if his mother had lost her mind. There was no one in the room and yet, the humming of voices filled the air.

Bina opened her eyes and turned to him. "You will get your answers, but we only have a small window of time."

The scraping of chairs against the tiled floor caught Harry's attention. Harry watched in awe as the chairs moved back as if people were pulling them back to sit in them. He could hear the voices and the shuffling of feet but couldn't see anyone.

"Come to the front with me, Harrell."

If his mother was referring to his given name, it meant that she expected no arguments. He followed her like the obedient child he once was.

Harry stood in front of the rows of empty chairs wondering what was going to happen next. The noise around them was increasing. He panned his gaze around the room and saw dark shadows moving, taking shape. The shapes that filled the room were out of focus and blurry one minute and had transformed into living, breathing, people the next. Or were they apparitions? They sat with their full attention on Bina.

"I thank you all for coming here on such short notice," she began. "If this is your first time here, I welcome you. I know you may find yourself completely confused and unsure of where you are. This is perfectly normal. I have awakened you from the drug-induced comas that GN doctors have been keeping you in. I've brought you all here to make you aware of the situation of the world we were part of and the new one waiting for us."

Harry wanted answers, but this was beyond what he was expecting. But then why would he be so shocked? He had no clue of what happened in Limbo land.

An Asian man, about 50-years old with dark hair peppered with grey, stood up. "Where are we and how did we get here?"

A small blonde woman in her early forties was the next to stand up and speak. "The last thing I remember was being questioned in the GN labs by Dr. Saeed and Dr. Jones. I was strapped to a chair. They were drilling me with questions about my daughter Serena."

Harry raised an eyebrow. Was this Serena's missing mother?

A large dark haired Caucasian man in his mid-40s, dressed in a wrinkled business suit interrupted. "You promised to help find my son Gabriel. I've been waiting patiently in my cell like you told us too. Have you found him?"

Harry sucked in his breath.

"We have found Gabriel. He is here with us but he is unaware of the reality of his situation," Bina said.

"What do you mean, Bina? And who is this person standing beside you?" he asked.

Bina turned to Harry and said, "Tell them."

Was she kidding? What was he supposed to say?

His mother touched his arm and pleaded with her eyes.

What was he supposed to say to them? Hey, everyone, Global Nation scientists have been performing tests on you on behalf of the demons who have been living among us. Oh wait... this would be a great intro... Welcome everyone to the land of the dead. You guys know you've passed on, right?

His mother jabbed her elbow into his arm.

He took a deep breath. "I'm Harry Doubt, Bina's son. I've been on a mission with my friends to find my mother and their missing loved ones."

Gabriel's father leaped to his feet. "You know where Gabriel is? Take me to him!"

Bina raised her hand and said, "Take a seat. You will see Gabriel in due time."

"Enough talk! We want answers! What is happening to us? Why can't we remember how we got here? Where is Gabriel?"

Before Harry could respond, Gabriel's father started rushing towards him plowing through the people in the rows in front of him.

The others in the room started standing up.

"Where is my daughter, Joanna?" the Asian man shouted.

The group of people started coming towards the front of the room, flickering in and out of focus.

Harry's mouth went dry and he could feel his heart pounding in his chest. He watched in horror as they glided toward him with anger in their eyes, their fists raised up as if to strike him.

Just then, Bina raised her arms up.

The furious ghost mob began fading out, their hands grasping and reaching out as if to grab hold of her until they disappeared.

"Don't send us back. Please let us stay here!" were the cries that were left echoing in the room.

Bina's arms fell limp and she stood very still. Harry grabbed her as she collapsed in his arms. He helped her sit down on a chair.

"Mom, are you okay?"

She gave him a weak smile. "I'm fine. Just got the wind knocked out of me, so to speak," she said.

Harry paced back and forth, trying to piece together everything he had just learned. His mind was racing and he couldn't make sense of any of it. Finally one thought entered his head. *Focus on the mission.*

He took his mother's hands in his and looked into her eyes.

"We need to get you and Carlos home. That was my mission and we have to leave now."

Bina's eyes grew wide as she looked past Harry's shoulder.

Harry turned to see who or what was behind him.

In the doorway, Carlos and Gabriel were standing just inside the doorframe. Carlos' eyes were wide as saucers and his hands were behind his back. Gabriel, on the other hand, was staring at him with a lost look as if he were in a daze.

But what made Harry's gut twist into knots was who was standing behind them: a tough looking guy with a smug grin on his face.

"Harry, never thought I'd see you on this side of the worlds."

Kerim Ilgaz, Harry's former head of security, stood with his six-foot high silver wings spread out behind him. He gave him a cold, triumphant smirk before shoving Carlos and Gabriel into the room.

CHAPTER 5
CROSSING BACK

Harry wasn't sure what to expect next. He glanced over at his mother. Her eyes narrowed and her lips pressed tight together. She seemed to be analyzing the situation.

Kerim was casing the room, a skilled security agent, checking to see if it was clear (of what, Harry wasn't entirely sure).

Carlos did not move from the spot where Kerim had left him. Sweat was pouring from his brow. Harry noticed Carlos shifting his weight from one leg to the other. It was a clear sign of Carlos' nervousness but again Harry was unsure why.

One thing he was sure of, he wasn't just going to stand there doing dick all.

Kerim sauntered toward Harry.

"The room is clear. We don't have much time," Kerim said.

Harry marched up to Kerim, grabbing his jacket in both fists.

"Who the hell do you think you are? You don't come here shoving Gabriel around or tying up Cristal's dad like they're criminals!"

Kerim gave him a cool smile, not flinching despite Harry's attempts to shake some sense into him.

"Let go of me, Harry. You're not my boss anymore," Kerim said with an icy glare.

Harry released Kerim and stepped back. *Keep calm.*

Bina came over to Harry and patted him on the shoulder, her way of telling him to take it down a notch.

She looked up at Kerim with a calm expression on her face. "I saw you in my dreams. You are a good angel, are you not?" she asked.

Kerim's eyebrows rose, his cheeky smile fading. Harry wished he could knock that smile right off his face.

Bina touched Kerim on the arm. He jumped back as if her hand had passed an electrical current through him.

"What was that?" Kerim said.

Bina stepped closer to him. "I know all about this place. It is very special. Megiddo is where all the worlds overlap. It is where the final battle will take place between the armies of the Beast and God to determine mankind's destiny," she said in a gentle voice.

Kerim eyed her closely before taking another step back. "Is this Sunday school, Bina?" he said, his voice wavering.

Bina glanced over at Carlos and tapped her right index finger on the side of her leg. The invisible power holding Carlos' hands behind his back was broken.

Carlos rubbed his wrists. "Bina, be careful," he said.

Harry stared at his mother with a new respect. He never knew she could be so tough.

She focused her attention at Kerim. "It is he who should be careful, Carlos. Megiddo is off limits for spirits to use their powers. Demons and angels know that if they break this law they could start the battle to end all battles," she said, taking another step closer to Kerim.

Kerim stumbled back. "Hey, lady. I'm here to help bring Harry back to the other side. Stop making this harder for me," he said.

Harry noted the anxiety in Kerim's voice.

Gabriel, who had been standing still watching everyone, seemed to come back to life. He strode over to Harry, shoving him down into a chair.

"Why didn't you tell me?" Gabriel shrieked.

Did Kerim tell him?

"I was going to," Harry sputtered, "but I wasn't sure if it was safe to tell you. I don't know much about the after-life. I wasn't sure what would happen if I told you that you were dead."

Gabriel's eyes widened, his jaw dropping. The air around them seemed to constrict and expand. Wooshing sounds swirled around them.

Harry glanced at Kerim, who shot him a fiery glare. He realized he had said too much.

Gabriel said, his voice rising, "What do you mean dead? Kerim told me that he was an angel and that you and I crossed over to Limbo after chasing him."

Harry stared in disbelief at Gabriel's chest where bullet holes were forming and blood was spilling out. Dark shadows manifested themselves around Gabriel, their outstretched arms reaching out to grab him.

Harry jumped out of the chair and ran towards him.

"Kerim, do something!" he said.

"I can't. Your mother is right. If I try to do anything, it will start a war that we're not ready to fight."

Harry couldn't believe his ears. He grabbed Gabriel, blocking him from the dark shadows that were lashing out. The sound of

ANNE-RAE VASQUEZ

their hissing and wailing echoed around them. He felt their claw-like fingers grasping his clothes.

"You're gonna be fine, Gabriel," he said.

"I remember now," Gabriel said, his voice a whisper while his body went limp in Harry's arms.

"Resist, Gabriel. Don't give up," Harry said. He let Gabriel's full weight lean on him.

The room started to shake from the ceiling down to the ground. Harry looked up to see Kerim and Bina holding hands. A blinding white light radiated from Kerim's body, the rays scorching the dark shadows clustered around Harry and Gabriel.

God-awful shrieks pierced the air as the shadows pulled away. A force was drawing them into the walls. The shadows closest to Kerim burned up into smoke and the few that managed to survive were sucked into the walls.

Harry could see Carlos kneeling on the ground, his hands clasped together as if in prayer. His right index finger touched the ground in front of him, tapping three times. It was like how he tapped the table in the restaurant earlier.

The sound around them escalated like the roar of a tornado on a rampage.

"What's happening?" Gabriel asked, his words so soft Harry could barely hear him.

"Not sure but hang on, okay?"

Harry supported Gabriel, who felt like a bag of feathers. He half dragged Gabriel towards Kerim and his mother.

The white light might be the way back.

Bina's eyes widened as Harry came closer to them.

"Mom, let's go back. If we all step into the white light, it will take us back."

32

Kerim shook his head and released Bina's hand. The bright white light vanished, snuffed out.

The somber expression on Kerim's face told Harry that there was more information to be revealed.

"Only you can go back, Harry," Kerim said. "Only the living can go back to the land of the living."

Harry frowned. His heart was beating so loud that he was sure the sound could have burst his eardrums. "I don't know what you mean!"

Gabriel shifted. "I want to go back," he gasped.

Harry glanced down. "Hang on."

Bina came over to them, placing her hand on Gabriel's forehead. Her touch seemed to have renewed his energy.

"I think I'm okay now. I can stand," he said.

Harry turned to his mother. "Mom, we have to go. We don't belong here. The mission was to bring you and Cristal's dad back."

Carlos looked up from his prayer-like position. "No, Harry," he said. "The mission is bigger than that. Bina and I are staying here. We will help prepare for the final battle. Mankind must resist the evil that is around them. They will feel lost and abandoned. Many will end up here. Your mother and I need to stay to help them learn the truth so that they can fight for the existence of humankind."

Harry's mind was reeling. Theology was one of the subjects he had avoided all his life. The little he knew was not enough to get him through this.

Bina touched his arm. "You need to go now. Carlos and I will open the portal. Go back with Kerim. He can take you safely to the other side."

Kerim stepped towards Harry, his wings expanding to their

full wingspan. "Your mother is right. We need to go soon. Raffe sent me here to take your mother and Carlos to the next part of their journey," he said. "But I understand their desire to resist. I was human too. Remember? Preserving mankind is not on the top of the Army's agenda right now. So much evil has destroyed humanity on Earth. The senior archangels like Raffe are reporting to the Commander-in-Chief that there is no hope for the future of humans. Humans have been given many chances to change their path but history proves over and over that the lessons of the past are meaningless."

Gabriel interrupted. "Commander-in-Chief?"

"You mortals refer to Him as the Almighty, Yahweh, Allah or God," Kerim said.

Harry gritted his teeth. "So you're saying that God wants to eradicate humans from the face of the earth?"

Kerim took a deep breath, glancing over at Gabriel who stared at him with defiance. "He has tried to do this in the past. You've probably heard the story of Sodom and Gomorrah, where God destroyed a city of sinners. And I'm sure you've heard of Noah's ark, right? Where God flooded the entire world? So yeah, you could say that."

"How about good people?" Gabriel asked. "There are tons of good people. Are you saying that your Commander-in-Chief is prepared to wipe them out too?"

Kerim's mouth twitched into a smile. "No. He has commanded the Army to bring the special ones here. It's a top-secret mission, under the code name *Rapture*."

A high-pitched sound blasted into the room from outside the window.

"It's time to go. Raffe and his army are outside." Kerim grabbed Harry's arm.

Harry turned to his mother. "Mom?"

She reached out and pulled him close to her. "Carlos and I will be fine. We will communicate with you when it is safe to."

She pressed something into Harry's hand. It was a black leather bracelet.

"Wear this on your way back," she said. She handed him a charm bracelet. "Give this to Cristal. She will need it to protect herself. No time to explain how."

Harry put the leather bracelet on his right wrist and slipped the charm bracelet in his pocket. He supposed they would have to figure out for themselves how the things work.

Tears were welling up in his eyes as he tried to fight to keep control of his emotions. "Mom, this isn't goodbye, is it?" he asked.

"It's never goodbye. We will be together again. Now go." Bina gave him a warm smile.

The high-pitched sound blasted through the room again.

Carlos yelled out. "Time to go, Harry. I'm going to tap the ground and the portal will open. Kerim will take you across. And Harry?"

"Yes, Carlos?"

"Take care of Cristal for me."

"Yes, always," Harry said.

Carlos closed his eyes, took a deep breath and touched his index finger to the ground. Bina knelt down beside him and touched the same spot with her index finger.

The floor started rippling in front of them.

Kerim grabbed Harry by the arm and pulled him to the center of the ripples.

Harry glanced to see Gabriel standing beside Bina, staring at him, eyes wide with fright.

Harry yanked his arm from Kerim's grip. He stepped towards

Gabriel, pulling him into the circle. The hard surface of the floor swayed.

"Gabriel, can't come with us!" Kerim said, pushing Gabriel back.

"He's coming with us, whether you like it or not!" Harry locked arms with Gabriel's.

The ground gave way just then, swallowing the three of them into a black hole of emptiness.

CHAPTER 6
TRAINING DAY

Cristal lifted her forearm, bracing herself for the impact. The kick to her side was blocked, but left her upper body vulnerable. Before she could duck, a flash of red rushed toward her face.

Bam!

She teetered backwards, hitting the mat on the ground behind her.

"Up!"

She lay there with her eyes shut, her muscles refusing to budge.

"Cristal! Get up!"

She forced her eyelids open, but even that hurt like hell. Standing above her was Serena, her friend and fight coach. Strands of blond hair poked through her headgear, her face streaked with drops of sweat.

"You know if you were in a real fight, you'd be dead right now," Serena said.

Cristal took a deep breath, turned over on her side and eased herself into a sitting position. She turned her head toward her, noting that even her neck muscles were screaming in pain.

"Technically, I could use my super blast power to blow them away," she managed to say.

Serena gave a big laugh and plopped herself down beside her. "Yeah, I guess you could do that," she replied. "But remember why you asked me to train you. You wanted to use your special powers only as a last resort."

Cristal grinned. "I know. I know. I just didn't think the training would be so tough. It's been eight weeks and I can't last even ten minutes on the mat with you."

Serena untied her headgear and yanked it off, placing it beside her. Cristal took hers off too, taking it as a sign that her coach was calling it a day.

Serena jumped up, turned and reached her hand out. "You're doing pretty damn well for someone just starting. I've been training for twelve years."

Good to know, she thought. She grabbed Serena's hand and pulled herself up.

Across the yard she could see Walid and his sisters standing at the bottom of the staircase watching them. Walid's mother let them use the cemented backyard for Serena's defense training. To show her support, Walid's mother helped sew together the exercise mats for them using old bed sheets stuffed with memory foam pieces.

Walid waved at her, flashing his white toothy smile. His sisters turned and started waving too.

Serena looked over her shoulder and smiled back. "Looks like your fans are cheering for you."

"Yeah, Walid's sisters make the best pain relieving salve," she said. "They can't wait to test it on me."

"Something smells good. Dinner must be ready," Serena said. "Let's go."

Cristal followed Serena, taking baby steps. The burn in her calf muscles reminded her of more training sessions to come. *No time to be a wuss.*

"Ms. Creestal," Walid said. He reached over to the small table beside him and picked up her cell phone. "Your phone rang."

Serena shot her a look.

The last time it rang was when Serena had contacted her the day after she arrived in Megiddo. She hadn't received another call since. Was it Harry?

She picked up her pace despite the pain that shot up her legs.

"Thanks Walid," she said as he handed her the phone.

Walid's sisters were listening, trying to translate English into Arabic between themselves.

Cristal checked her phone log. Joanna's name was listed as the last caller. She sensed Walid and Serena were watching her closely.

"It was Joanna," she said. Her phone vibrated in her hand.

One unread text message.

"Looks like she left a text with her alias Onyx."

She read the message aloud.

Onyx: NYC is a war zone. GN's trying to restore power. Sent multiple texts to Zero but no response. Not sure if you'll get this. Confirm receipt.

Walid frowned. "There is no Internet, and cell phones don't work since the earthquake. How come you get phone call and text message?"

Serena gave Cristal a look. Walid had been very hospitable

and helpful to both of them. The problem was that he wasn't an official Truth Seeker and this information was privileged data.

Earlier, Cristal and Serena had checked the Truth Seeker satellite network by pinging the underground servers that Harry had set up in secret locations all over the world. Serena pinged or sent a test file to all the servers and received confirmation that the messages were received successfully, confirming that all systems were up and running. She also sent messages out to her father in the Philippines and Cristal's mother in New York. They had yet to receive any reply.

Cristal cleared her throat. "Maybe the cell phone signal is picking up now."

"Oh? My phone has no signal." He held his phone out for her to see.

Serena said, "GN has a special data phone plan for its employees. Keeps us connected when natural disasters happen."

Walid raised his eyebrow then cracked a grin. "Can you turn on *Hotspot?*"

Serena and Cristal eyed each other before giggling. Cristal turned to Walid.

"Feel free to tether to my phone anytime," she said.

Walid translated this message to his sisters who proceeded to chatter to each other with excitement.

"Maybe we can try and build network here so we can connect with others outside of Megiddo," he said. "It's so difficult to travel to Haifa now that the roads are destroyed. My cousins who work with IDF and the government are rebuilding Haifa. They will help us connect to rest of world."

Cristal and Serena exchanged looks. "Of course," Serena said. "We'll help you build a network."

The sound of a woman's scream pierced the air.

"Immee?" Walid said, his eyes darting toward the house.

His sisters started scrambling up the stairs.

Serena grabbed a steel pipe which was sitting on top of a box of assorted old tools.

"Walid's mom is in trouble. Let's go."

CHAPTER 7
MAN WITH WINGS

Cristal was the last one to enter the room. In the corner, Walid was holding onto his mother, who was wailing at the top of her lungs.

He turned to Cristal. "She says she saw strange men here in the room. There was a white light over there near the TV set."

"No intruders as far as I can see," Serena said. She proceeded to sweep the room for anything suspicious.

Walid's sisters were standing in the hallway, peering in.

Shaima, the older one said, "I saw one of them on the stairs. A young man."

"I saw him too," the youngest said.

Cristal had not seen anyone pass her on the stairs. "Are you sure?"

The middle one nodded her head and pointed. "Yes. And the one with the wings is standing beside my mother."

Serena shot Cristal a look. They both turned towards Walid's mother.

Walid looked over to where his sister was pointing. "No one there," he said.

Cristal wasn't so sure. She approached the spot where the "man with wings" was supposedly standing. Every nerve in her body tingled as she sensed a weird vibration in the area beside Walid's mother.

"Be careful," Serena said, raising the pipe in her hand.

Cristal's senses were picking up more energy around her. She pointed at Walid.

"Take your mother and Serena out of the room."

Serena stepped towards Cristal, the pipe still in her hand. "I'm not going anywhere."

Walid helped his mother up and escorted her out. His sisters followed behind them, looking back in hopes of catching another glimpse of the uninvited guests.

Serena took a step towards Cristal. "What is it? Do you see anything?"

See anything? The answer was "no" but there was no doubt about it. Something was in the room with them. She closed her eyes to concentrate on finding what that something was.

With her eyes shut, the sound of voices surrounded her but the words were distant and muddled. After a few more seconds, her heightened senses picked up something else. The only way she could describe it to herself was that it was a wave of emotions. Fear. Panic.

"Cristal."

Her eyes flickered open.

Dad?

Serena stopped and turned towards her. "Did you see something?"

Cristal shook her head slowly. "Stay still," she said.

"What is it?"

Her eyes caught movement, glimmers of a shape of someone standing in front of her. Was she seeing things?

"Come on, what is it?" Serena asked.

Cristal reached out, freezing as the shape took on a more solid state. She sucked in her breath.

"Gabriel?"

It was impossible and yet there he was, standing in front of her exactly as he looked on the day he died, dreadlocks pulled back in a short ponytail and wearing the same long sleeve white T-shirt and baggy blue jeans. She noted there was no sign of bullet holes or blood on his shirt.

Serena walked up beside her. "Cristal, are you okay?"

Cristal felt the vibration in her joints increase in intensity, her body humming in harmony with the energy. It was like watching Gabriel through a looking glass. He seemed to be looking straight at her but she knew he couldn't see her.

"I see Gabriel," she said.

"What? Where?" Serena said.

The room began to expand and contract. Serena didn't react, oblivious of what Cristal was experiencing.

Cristal saw Gabriel's eyes were wide open as an arm reached out and pulled him toward her. More waves of energy rippled around him. The angle changed and she could see the upper body of the person who had pulled Gabriel. He turned his head in her direction. It was Harry!

"Cristal, tell me what you're seeing!" Serena said.

Cristal felt her teeth begin to ache as the vibrations in the room became stronger.

"I see Harry," she managed to say.

"What is happening? Where are they? Is Gabriel alive?"

Before she could reply, an intense bright white light exploded resembling a small bomb. The waves of energy sent Serena toppling backward.

Unlike Serena, Cristal was not shaken from the spot she was standing on. Her feet were rooted to the ground by a force similar to what happened at Akko, the day the white light blasted through her body.

Calmness swept over her even with the white light blasting from the floor to the ceiling. Her attention was focused on the dark shapes swirling in the center of the light.

Overwhelmed with the urge to speak, she said, "Come to me!"

Her voice boomed out with a thunderous roar.

As soon as the words left her lips, Gabriel stumbled into the room. Two seconds later Harry was standing beside him.

"Gabriel! Harry!" Serena cried out.

The white light began fading, making her wonder if the portal was closing. When Harry looked back over his shoulder she realized that the light wasn't fading at all. The light was being blocked out by something. A large cloud of mist with wings was flying straight towards her. The silver wings spanned about half the width of the room. As it flew, its shape morphed into human form, the wings remaining spread open.

As its face began to change, it was the eyes that gave his true identity away. They were the steel grey eyes that haunted her every night in her dreams. Kerim.

Before she could react, Harry called out to her. His voice was muffled by the sound of the vibrating energy reverberating against the walls.

She focused her energy on his words to make out what he was saying.

"Close the portal."

A dark shadow was emerging from behind Kerim, racing toward them.

"Close the portal!" This time the command was from Kerim.

Serena grabbed her by the arm. "Close the portal! There's something else coming over from the other side!"

Cristal switched gears and focused her energy toward the white light.

Serena pulled her arm again. "Can you hear me Cristal? Close the portal!"

She threw Serena a glare and snapped. "Dammit! Can't you see that's what I'm trying to do?"

The room became very still while a cloud of darkness fell upon them. She spun back toward the portal.

Blocking out the light was something double the size of Kerim; its golden wings outstretched a good twenty feet, reaching from one wall to the other across the width of the room. She recognized its eyes, dark as pools of liquid ink even before it started to take its human form.

She realized that her life was in grave danger.

CHAPTER 8
RESIST

In a matter of seconds, the giant cloud of mist transformed into its human form – a short stocky Mediterranean looking man with dark wavy hair and a fierce expression on his face. His wings remained outstretched as visual proof of his power. Was it to remind them that he was Archangel Rafael? But to Cristal, he was still just Raffe—Kerim's strange friend.

"Here you are, Cristal Hernandez," he said, his voice booming like a thunderclap. "I knew that if I followed this band of buffoons, it would lead straight to you."

Now he thinks he's a comedian.

Cristal swallowed hard as she scanned the room. Did the Truth Seekers have an idea of what to do next?

She noticed that Kerim's stare was fixed on her. Chances were he was reading her thoughts again.

She glanced over to see Gabriel hide behind Kerim, shielding himself from Raffe. She had played enough online games with him to know that he was sensing impending danger.

Serena poked her in the arm. "Zero is sending a message," she mumbled.

Cristal looked over to see Harry tapping his finger on his leg. Morse code. It was how he communicated with her while playing online games.

..... / -.-. .- -. .---. - / .... .- -. - / -.-- --- ..- / .... . .-. . .-.-

The message said: He can't hurt you here.

At that moment, Kerim rushed towards Harry, grabbing him by his jacket and hurling him to the ground.

Did he hear my thoughts? she asked herself.

"Oh yeah?" Kerim said as he pinned Harry down with his foot. "Tell me, Zero. Does this hurt?"

"Get off of me!" Harry thrashed his arms and legs, trying to free himself.

Without warning, Gabriel came from behind and rushed towards Kerim with both his fists up.

Kerim twisted his body, avoiding the hit. With a swift move, he grabbed Gabriel by the arm and threw him across the room.

Gabriel slammed against the wall and landed on the floor.

Serena whispered to her. "Do something or I will."

Let's see how tough you are, Kerim, Cristal thought to herself.

She ran towards him and attacked him with a sweep kick, quickly twisting her hip and directing the side of her shin into his shin, throwing him off balance.

"Get away from here, Harry! I got this covered," she said as she pulled her knee up and backwards, striking Kerim in the knees with the ball of her foot, toppling him to the ground.

Harry jumped up, his mouth open in shock.

"Damn! You go, girl!" Serena called out.

Cristal knew that she had to take Kerim out fast before he had the chance to regain his senses. Bending her knee, she quickly extended her leg up and downwards, giving Kerim a foot-thrust kick to his neck.

Kerim was disabled for the time being. She left him motionless on the ground, backing away with her fists held close to her face, ready to defend herself with deadly punches if needed.

"Very good performance."

Cristal's eyes snapped upwards to catch Raffe clapping his hands. He had watched their antics with a bemused expression. The sneer on his face seemed to dare her to punch him.

"Leave me and my friends alone," she said.

The vibrations from deep inside the core of her body pulsated in controlled but powerful waves around her.

Kerim groaned as he scrambled to sit up.

Poor Kerim. Cristal had used her special powers to add force to her kicks. Who would blame her? This was war, and if you want to win the fight you have to fight with equivalent or stronger force. Serena had always told her to fight dirty if needed.

Raffe sauntered over to Cristal, his wings stretching out wider than before.

"Friends? Don't friends sway their loyalty and become lethal enemies in, how you say, a blink of an eye?" His words swirled around her head, like a lizard's tongue flickering, teasing and taunting her.

She could sense Serena and Harry beside her. Gabriel was unmistakably close by too. His aura was releasing surges of fear and anger. Something must have happened to him on the other side, but now wasn't the time to ponder the details.

Harry made the first move, stepping in front of Raffe. "We are not afraid of you," he said with a steady voice.

Raffe's gaze raked over him with disdain. "But you **should** be afraid, little mortal." His lips curled into a chilling smirk.

Harry's left hand was shaking, which meant his bravado was all a dramatic bluff. She had noticed his hand shake the day Gabriel died, when he was holding out his phone for her to watch the video that revealed Kerim's true identity.

Raffe sighed and turned towards Cristal dismissing Harry's challenge as nothing more than a distraction, an annoyance.

"You are an interesting one indeed," he said, advancing towards her.

Serena crossed into his path, raising the pipe above her shoulder ready to strike.

"Let us go," she said.

Raffe raised an eyebrow, pausing to speak. "Tick tock. Time is running out for you, little lady. It's running out for your friends. For mankind."

Serena spread her feet apart; knees bent preparing for her next move.

"Everyone step back," Cristal said.

Raffe clapped his hands together generating a deafening sound.

"You heard the girl," he said. The wave of his hand sent an invisible force shoving Serena and Harry off to either side creating an opening for him to pass.

Serena and Harry gave each other a "what just happened" look.

Raffe continued walking towards Cristal.

"You freakin' jerk!" she said.

"Now, now, that's not very nice," he said. He lifted his hand, the palm facing her.

She focused her thoughts on the energy inside of her, not taking time to deduce whether he was going to shoot first, talk later. *Knock this Raffe onto his ass. You can do it.*

She pointed her hands towards him, the energy shaking every muscle in her body. Her arms began to throb and beams of smoking white light blasted out from her hands directly at Raffe's chest.

The blast threw him a few steps backward and for a millisecond his eyes widened in surprise.

"Cristal!" Harry cried out.

Raffe lifted himself off the ground, flapping his wings and building up speed in her direction—an angry bull charging towards the matador's red cape.

Cristal funneled the power from the core of her body and pointed her hands towards Raffe again, sending more energy— blast after blast.

Although each hit seemed to help decelerate his speed, it didn't hinder him from surging forward, as if making up for lost ground.

The more determined he seemed, the more energy Cristal summoned. Her natural stubbornness mixed with her blind faith in Harry gave her the will to fight. *He can't hurt me here.*

Raffe stopped and hovered, looming in front of her, his human form dwarfed out by the gargantuan wings behind him. It was an odd sight to say the least.

"Cristal!" The thunderous roar emanating from Raffe's lips muted Serena and Harry's screams, snapping Cristal back to the event at hand.

"In the name of the Almighty One," Raffe continued, "I command you to..."

Before he could finish, Cristal was shoved to the side with a huge force, causing her to collide into Serena and Harry. She landed on the ground, skidding to a stop.

CHAPTER 9
BETRAYED

C ristal didn't have time to figure out what hit her. She looked up to see Kerim holding a shining silver sword that was pointed dead center at Raffe's chest. The shaft was covered with ornate drawings—golden light seeped out of the swirls and symbols.

Serena held out her hand for Cristal to grab. "We have to get the hell out of here," she said.

"Yes," Harry said. "While those two are distracted."

Cristal gripped Serena's hand and pulled herself up.

Raffe's roar shook the room. "You dare wave your sword at me?"

Kerim raised his left hand. "It's only drawn in case this doesn't work." A blast of white light shot out of his hand into Raffe's face, catapulting him backward into the portal.

Cristal said, "Now's our chance. Let's go." She noticed Gabriel off to the side, his eyes glued to the scene unfolding.

"Gabriel," she called out. "We have to go! Now!"

He turned, nodded his head and ran towards them. "Cristal it's so good to see you again," he said.

She patted him on the arm. "You too."

Harry yelled out over the roar of the battle cries erupting from Raffe and Kerim's mouths. Weren't angels supposed to speak in whispers, lounge on a bed of clouds eating dark chocolate and playing harps?

"Cristal, put this on! My mother said that it'll help," Harry said, snapping her back to her senses.

He handed her a bracelet with miniature charms dangling from it. Among the myriad of charms the following ones caught her eye: triple silver hearts, a key, a magnifying glass and a globe.

She slipped the bracelet onto her wrist. "Did she say how to use it?"

He shook his head. "No, but we'll figure it out later."

Serena said, "Okay, so what next guys? The angel battle isn't going to last forever."

Cristal's wrist began throbbing as if a source of energy was coming from the charm bracelet. She glanced down to see that the globe charm was glowing a blue light.

"I think we have our answer," she said. The joints in her arms and hands began vibrating.

Harry lifted his wrist revealing a black leather braided bracelet which was glowing with a reddish light.

"My finger is pulsing. Is yours?" he asked.

She realized that her finger *was* pulsing. "Yeah, it is. It's like it has a mind of its own."

Gabriel pointed to the ground where a puddle of water appeared before his feet. The floor seemed to be rippling open in small circular waves.

"On the other side, Rose and Roberto tapped the ground to teleport us out. Maybe that's what you guys have to do," he said.

Who the heck were Rose and Roberto?

Harry grabbed Cristal's arm. "Yes, let's both touch the ground." They knelt down together.

Cristal's joints were buzzing with electrical energy. Her finger was drawn to the same spot on the ground Harry's finger was touching.

Serena whispered, "The globe on your bracelet is glowing brighter."

"Tap three times," Harry said.

He didn't need to tell her that as it seemed her finger was tapping the ground on autopilot.

Tap. Tap. Ta---

"Cristal!" Raffe cried out.

Startled by the sound, she glanced up.

Hovering above her was Kerim, his silvery wings outstretched.

"Come with me Cristal," he said in a voice that was not his own.

"Kerim?" she said.

"Let's go together," his voice hummed in her ear. "We can be together forever. Far away from everyone."

Cristal's heart was pounding hard and it seemed for a moment that it was only she and Kerim in the room. Everything else around her stood still, even though she and Kerim were in motion. Was this how the character Hiro in the TV show *Heroes* manipulated the space-time continuum?

"I've missed you," she heard herself say but no sound escaped from her lips.

Kerim smiled, his grey eyes shining. "As I have missed you." He reached out his hand. "Take it. Time is running out."

How she wanted to grab his hand but one thought entered her mind slicing through her euphoric daze.

TGTBT

It was the Truth Seekers' code. *Too good to be true.*

"Cristal!"

She heard the simultaneous screams from Harry, Serena and Gabriel. She blinked hard. Was she seeing things?

Kerim smiled as he hovered in front of her. She sucked in her breath. The glint of shiny metal flashed as he waved his sword in the air.

CHAPTER 10
TELEPORTATION

C ristal realized that the tip of Kerim's sword was rushing straight toward her chest.

Just then Gabriel grabbed her wrist and yanked her to the ground.

"Tap the ground!" he yelled.

That was her intention, but her hand was a brick of lead. "I think Kerim's stopping me," she said.

"I'll change that," he said.

He took her hand and tapped her index finger to the ground.

Waves of energy vibrated from inside her in outward arcs, creating a dome-like translucent shield five feet around her.

The tip of Kerim's sword bounced off as if hitting an indestructible wall.

"Gabriel, good job," Harry said, giving him a pat on his shoulder. He whipped around towards Cristal. "Are you okay?"

The ground gave way before she could respond. It felt like she was standing on a wet sponge and the only thing keeping her from falling into an endless black pit was to steady herself on a giant wave as the ground rippled open beneath her.

"Let's go!" Harry said as he put his arm around her, bringing her closer to him. Gabriel and Serena jumped into the portal with Cristal and Harry following behind them. The shield of energy around them was protecting them. For now.

She turned back to Harry, who was fading into molecular dust before her eyes.

The cells in her body were humming in synch with the vibrations that were still pulsing out of her. Glancing down, she watched her hands disintegrate into nothingness. She heard the loud flap of wings that could have been mistaken for the sound of giant birds swooping down to prey on an unknowing mouse scavenging for food on the ground.

"Don't look back," Harry said.

Despite his warning, Cristal turned and looked over her shoulder. An old memory from her weekly Catechism classes about the Biblical story of Sodom and Gomorrah surfaced, when Lot's wife looked back against the angels' orders and turned into a pillar of salt.

Although she hadn't turned into a pile of salt, she regretted not listening to Harry.

Kerim was hovering above her, the sadness in his eyes made her heart twist into knots.

Never doubt me, his voice said in her head.

Behind him she could see the gold tips of Raffe's wings. Kerim turned, raising his sword in the air.

"The Almighty One has condemned you to fall. You are no longer in His graces." Raffe's voice boomed into the air.

Cristal held her breath. Raffe raised his hands emitting bluish streaks of light. The blades of light sliced into Kerim's body.

"Ahhhh!" Kerim's painful cry sent shivers down her arms.

The roar of the heavens joined the hair-raising scream.

The sound dissipated, fading into the distance as Cristal and the Truth Seekers slipped into the blackness. They were suspended in a dark vacuum which was absent of light and external sounds. And yet they could see each other and hear each other. How was this possible?

"The portal's closed," Harry said.

"Those angel freaks can't follow us. Can they?" Gabriel said.

Serena's eyebrows shot up and gave Cristal a look.

Cristal turned to Harry. "Can they?"

Harry floated towards them. "I think we're okay. Lucky for us Raffe's mission to destroy Cristal shifted to Kerim."

Cristal's stomach churned while the memory of Kerim being sliced into pieces by Raffe's energy blast replayed in her mind.

"Are you okay?" Serena said, reaching out to her.

Cristal nodded. "Yeah, I'm fine." But she was far from being fine.

She turned to Harry. "Do you know how long it takes before we get to our next stop?"

Harry glanced briefly at Gabriel before answering. "Next stop? This is all new for me too."

Serena interrupted. "Do you even know what the next stop is?"

Cristal noticed Harry's expression grow dark.

A jolt of energy wrapped around her wrist. The bracelet! She lifted her arm.

"Guys, the globe on the bracelet is spinning like crazy," she said.

Harry floated closer to her and lifted his wrist. The leather bracelet he was wearing was glowing bright blue.

"Cristal," he said, waving to her. "Maybe you can choose our next destination."

Gabriel interrupted. "Yes, of course! Rose said that the bracelet would help Cristal."

Cristal touched the map on the globe. The map peeled off the globe and magnified in front of them. They were now staring at a hologram.

"Gabriel's right!" Harry said. "You can probably choose anywhere on the map, Cristal."

There was only one place she wanted to go. She reached out and touched the map—New York.

CHAPTER 11
NEW YORK

C ristal found herself freefalling through what seemed to be a timeless warp, a vacuum of emptiness where nothing visual or audible could help measure the speed of her descent or determine how hard the impact would be when she landed. Part of her wondered if the individual atoms in her body were travelling on their own, grouped together by her spiritual being.

Her thoughts disintegrated as she landed flat on her back into a mountain of feathers or what seemed like it. The fluffy cotton texture caressed her cheeks while her hands grasped clumps of pillowy softness between her fingers. *Could this be Kerim's wings catching her from the fall?*

Before she could collect her thoughts, a bright ray of light flashed above her, followed by a dark figure plummeting down from above her. Cristal rolled away seconds before becoming a human quesadilla, bumping into a large object which had that unmistakable smell of new leather.

A large crash behind her caused her to turn and look over her shoulder but the darkness made it difficult to see who had just tumbled into the room.

"Are you okay?" she asked.

"Ugh," came the reply. The grunt was from Harry. It was the same sound he made when she challenged him about his theories.

She pulled herself into a sitting position as she noted the surroundings. They had landed inside a small apartment. The flooring was covered in a light colored shag carpet and not a pile of feathers as she'd earlier assumed. The feeling of *déjà vu* hit her after she scanned the room.

"Yeah, I'm okay," Harry said, standing up and surveying the room.

Another flash of light came from the ceiling, followed by a rumbling noise.

Harry reached his hand out for her to grab. "Better get out of the way."

She grabbed it, stood up in time for them to both scramble to the side when it dawned on her where they were.

"Gabriel's apartment," she said.

Harry looked around. "Oh yeah, that's right. Guess Gabriel's choice of shag carpeting came in handy today." He gave her a wink.

She looked up and saw that a circular shape in the ceiling was expanding in waves, rippling outward in circles.

"They should be landing here soon," he said.

She anticipated Serena and Gabriel tumbling down through the portal above them. The ceiling began to bulge while the noise around them grew. It reminded her of the birth of a calf which she witnessed when she was a child visiting a family farm in Mexico.

Four feet appeared through the opening. Then two sets of

legs. But instead of barreling down as Cristal and Harry had done just minutes earlier, Serena and Gabriel floated into the middle of the living room like ballet dancers landing from a *Grand Jete* leap. It would have been a beautiful sight to see on stage but here and now, Cristal could only wonder what was going to happen next.

"Now how did they do that?" she said under her breath.

"Good question," Harry replied. "I'm planning to ask them."

Serena was doing her usual panning around the room and screening her surroundings before turning to them. Gabriel, on the other hand, reached out and gave Serena a big hug. Still holding on to her, he danced in a circle.

"Home! I'm home," he said.

"Stop it!" Serena said, pushing him back with a smile. "I'm getting dizzy."

Gabriel released her from his grip. "Sorry about that."

Serena turned and gave them a thumbs up. "Mission was a success. Cristal got us here all in one piece."

Cristal walked over to her with Harry by her side.

"Yeah, the charm bracelet is very useful," Harry said. He headed to the window and peeked through the blinds.

"How is it out there?" Gabriel asked.

When Harry did not respond, Serena shot Cristal a look.

"Guess, it must be pretty bad," she said. "Let's see how bad."

Part of Cristal wanted to stay put. Play dumb. Pretend that everything was fine. But the Truth Seeker in her drew her towards the window to see for herself what devastation the earthquake had caused. The earthquake she had inadvertently started.

Gabriel walked past her and stood beside Harry and Serena. For a brief second, his body became translucent, the sight of which made her shiver since technically Gabriel was still dead. Maybe it didn't seem that way in the place where both the spiritual and the living world cross. But how about outside the places where the worlds didn't overlap? Would he be a ghost to other people? She shook the questions from her head. It was time to focus on the here and now.

"It's awful," she heard Gabriel whisper.

Cristal took a step forward and peeked through the slat.

She sucked in her breath. The high-rise buildings that she expected to see were nothing more than mountains of rubble; the street was littered with abandoned cars and buses. Worst yet was the lack of people on the street.

"My God. Did I do this?" she said, turning away from the window. The room began spinning around her and she reached out her hands to regain her balance.

Gabriel tried to grab her but his hands went through her body. "What the—?" he said.

Was she nothing more than a group of atoms held together by a magnetic force? She felt the same way when they were transporting over from Megiddo to New York.

She could hear Serena gasp. "Harry, something is happening with Cristal."

"What do you mean?" Cristal turned towards them.

"You're glowing," Harry said.

She looked down to see that her body was emitting a soft white light. "I don't feel so good," she mumbled.

"Wait a minute," he said. "You may be standing on the spot where both worlds overlap." Harry came closer to her. "Focus your energy and move away from that spot. Come towards me."

"Okay. I'll try," she said. She closed her eyes and pushed all her thoughts towards Harry's direction. She lifted her left leg; the energy swirled around her like waves. Each movement was heavy and slow as the waves pushed against her body. *Got to get off this spot.*

She took another step. As her foot touched the ground, the magnetic energy released her from its grip, keeling her forward into Harry's arms.

"Let's get you to the couch," Harry said.

Serena grabbed her around the waist and began steering her.

Serena's touch sent a jolt through Cristal, lifting the dizziness from her and leaving her feeling revived.

"Let go. I'm fine," Cristal said.

"Are you sure?" Harry asked.

She flashed him a smile and pulled away from his arms.

"Yes, I am feeling great...and hungry." She turned to Gabriel. "You got anything we could eat? I'm famished."

The three of them stared at her.

"Why are you staring at me?" she asked.

Gabriel cracked a grin. "I'm sure we've got some canned food in the cupboards." He disappeared into the kitchen.

Serena walked over to the side table and reached for the lamp.

"I doubt that there would be power," Harry said.

"Well, we'll never know unless we try," she replied. She flipped the switch and white light filled the room.

Serena eyes widened. "So the electricity is working."

Gabriel stuck his head back into the living room. "Yeah, and the freezer is still working. I'm going to throw some steaks on the grill."

Serena, Harry and Cristal looked at each other.

"Do dead people eat?" Serena whispered.

"Shh! He might hear you," Cristal said.

Harry shrugged his shoulders. "You know, nothing makes sense to me anymore. Maybe here in this place, Gabriel is as human as you and me. Not sure what happens when he steps outside the door or outside the building."

Cristal shivered recalling Gabriel as a see-through apparition when he stood close to the window earlier.

"What are you guys whispering about?" Gabriel said, carrying a tray of drinks into the room.

Serena went over to him. "Let me help you. Man, I'm famished. It seems like we haven't eaten in days."

Harry sat down on the couch. "Well, who knows how long in human days we were transporting over from Megiddo?"

Cristal sat down beside him pulling out her cell phone from her pocket. "Oh, you're right. It's been seven days since we left!"

"Harry, did you try to get a hold of Joanna?" Serena said.

"I texted her a few minutes ago."

"And?" Cristal asked.

"And... she hasn't texted back yet."

Gabriel opened his laptop on the coffee table. "Okay, I'm going to hack into GN." He grabbed a glass and took a sip. "Maybe it's not as bad as we think."

Cristal stared as the water poured into his mouth, travelled down through his body, spilling into a pool onto the couch. Gabriel's torso was partially transparent, the black leather from the couch seeping through him.

No one else seemed to notice.

CHAPTER 12
CHARM BRACELET

Gabriel opened the web browser on his laptop. The screen came up to a blank page. She had expected to see a "404" or even a "Not found" error message. Odd.

"Google is down," he said.

Serena moved closer to the screen. "You're connected to the satellite network, right? Are you saying that Google is down or is the Internet down?"

Harry said, "Bet you Global Nation's website is up."

Serena turned and shot Cristal a glance. She mouthed "Did you tell him about Joanna's text?"

Harry sat back, his gaze meeting Cristal's.

"Tell me about what?" he said.

She took a deep breath. "Guess with all the excitement, I forgot to mention that Joanna sent me a text when we were in Megiddo."

"And..." he said.

She reached into her pocket and brought out her cell phone.

"She said that New York was a war zone and that GN was trying to restore power."

Gabriel faced them and smiled. "Well, this confirms that GN is up and running."

The GN website filled the screen.

"Let me have a look," Harry said. He tapped the trackpad, which brought up a video player in a light box. Underneath the caption read, "Eye witness reports."

He clicked the play button, drumming the table with his left hand as he waited.

The video was shaking. Panicked screams, grey plumes of smoke and tall licks of flames filled the screen. Sounds of angry alarms blared.

A voice behind the camera cut through the screams.

"Oh my God," a woman said in what sounded more like a gasp than words.

Another voice. "The buildings are gone."

The video shifted upwards with blood red clouds swirling the sky.

"We got to go! Now!"

A loud crack of thunder blasted in the air, followed by streaks of neon white lightning flashed into the sky. More screams followed. The picture shook sharply from side to side. The screen went black.

The next video loaded into the player. The picture was dark and fuzzy. Shrieks and wails blared out from the speakers. Cristal held her breath as the images began to sharpen.

On the screen, she could see a pair of small sneakers sticking out from under a mangled pile of metal. Two men appeared to be trying to lift the metal piece by piece.

"My baby! Please help!" The child's mother was on her knees.

"Put your damn phone away and help!" a voice behind the camera yelled.

The picture shook up and down, then side to side.

"Let go of me!"

"The world is coming to an end and all you can do is film it happening?"

An explosion cut through the screams. The picture of the ground spun several times before going black.

Serena stood up and turned away, clutching her stomach with one hand and covering her mouth with the other.

"Are you okay?" Cristal asked, rushing to her side. "Maybe you should sit down."

Serena shook her head. "I need to contact my dad. I hope he's okay."

Cristal helped her down on the couch. "Yeah, I was thinking about my mom too. We can try to reach them when we go to Global Nation tomorrow. We should stop watching videos for tonight."

She turned. "Right, Harry?"

He looked over his shoulder. "Gabriel and I need to figure out exactly what happened. We'll lower the volume down."

Serena struggled to get up. "It's okay, Cristal. I feel better now."

Cristal placed her hand on her shoulder and gently pushed her back down. There was a tingling sensation from the bracelet around her wrist. She felt a pulse of energy go through her hand to Serena's shoulder.

"No. You rest. We can save the world tomorrow. Right now, take it easy."

Serena shivered for a second. "Whoa. What was that?"

"Electric shock?"

"I don't think so," Serena said. She looked down at her body and grinned. "I feel fantastic." She leaped up and stood beside her.

"Something just happened here," Cristal said.

"Definitely. It must be the bracelet. It felt like you gave me some of your power."

Harry and Gabriel had joined them, excitement in their eyes.

"Transference of power. Cool!" Gabriel said.

Cristal lifted her arm to show them that the bracelet was no longer emitting energy. It had become an ordinary piece of jewelry.

Harry came close to inspect it. "I believe that if we made another bracelet, we could duplicate the energy into that."

"Maybe that's how your mom made your bracelet," Gabriel said.

Cristal turned to Harry. "Your mom?" He had not once mentioned anything about finding his mother. What else had he not told them?

"Oh and your dad," Gabriel said to her.

"My dad?" Her heart skipped a beat. "You found my dad? Where is he? Why didn't they come back with you?"

Harry took a deep breath. "It's a bit complicated."

Serena interrupted. "Just tell us what happened over there on the other side."

"I think we're all going to have to sit down for this," Gabriel said.

Harry grabbed Cristal's hand, catching her off guard.

"I tried to complete my mission to bring them back," he said, his voice filled with emotion.

The look in his eyes made her realize he knew something that he wasn't willing to admit.

CHAPTER 13
PUZZLE PIECES

Harry spoke in a soft tone, at times rushing through the points. His eyes avoided looking into theirs when he described the strange meeting of spirits his mother had conjured up on the other side. His constant pauses and "um's" were a clear sign that he was finding the story difficult to share. When she realized that the "spirits" he was referring to were actually their friends' missing loved ones, she finally understood Harry's strange behavior.

"My mom? Is she okay?" Serena cried out when she heard that her mother was one of the ghostly attendees.

Harry nodded, not meeting her gaze. "Like I said, all of them looked okay. But they entered the room like they were ghosts." He glanced over at Gabriel who seemed dazed by the story.

"What do you mean ghosts?" Serena asked. "Are you saying that my mom is dead?" Tears sprung to her eyes.

Gabriel shifted in his seat. "It's okay, Serena." He reached out and patted her on the shoulder. "Being dead isn't that bad."

Serena glanced up, her gaze meeting his. "I'm sorry. I forgot that..." She paused, at a loss for words.

He shrugged. "Yeah, well. Just letting everyone know, I haven't forgotten."

Cristal looked over at Harry, unsure of what to say or if she should say anything. "Say something," she mouthed to him.

Harry narrowed his eyes. "This is new for me too."

Gabriel said, "Yeah, I know."

Cristal couldn't take it anymore. "We have to go to GN to find out what's going on."

"But you said our parents are at the GN in Israel," Serena said. "Shouldn't we find them there instead of here?" Her frantic stare met Cristal's.

Serena's suggestion did make sense. Cristal was about to comment when the charm bracelet began vibrating around her wrist. She lifted her arm up to take a closer look.

"Hey, your bracelet is glowing again," Gabriel said, pointing at it.

Serena moved closer to her. "The charm that looks like a rectangle is glowing."

"Let me see that," Harry said, moving closer to see as well. "The charms look like they're shaking."

The bracelet was gently vibrating in short pulses. She said, "It's more like 'vibrating' like a cell phone."

Harry motioned with his hand. "Cristal, you're on to something. Maybe it's working like a cell phone."

"Touch it and see what happens," Serena said.

Cristal touched the rectangle, the glowing light peeled off and magnified in front of them resembling a floating 46-inch translucent screen. The blue light flickered, followed by the sound of crackling. After a few seconds the shape of a person began to materialize onto the screen. Cristal held her breath, half hoping and half knowing whom the person might be.

The picture was out of focus and the sound of the voice was muffled.

Concentrate and pick up the signal, she told herself while closing her eyes. *Focus.*

"Roberto!" She heard Gabriel cry out.

Roberto? She'd hoped it would be Carlos, her father.

"Cristal."

Her eyes snapped open.

Her heart skipped a beat. "Dad?" She managed to say as tears sprung to her eyes.

So much time had passed. His dark brown eyes were etched with wrinkles and his crooked smile made him look both sad and happy at the same time.

"My darling, I've waited so long for this moment," he said, his voice wavering.

She felt Harry's hand grasp hers. Her instinct was to shake it away but the comfort of his touch seemed to calm her senses.

He leaned over and whispered, "The picture is getting clearer when we hold hands."

Harry was right about that. Her father looked vivid enough for her to reach out and touch him.

"Cristal, not sure how much time we have," her father said. He glanced over his shoulder before turning back to her.

"Carlos," Harry said. "Are you and my mom okay?"

His eyebrows twisted into a knot. "We've been one step ahead of the Archangel Rafael. Bina is using her power to shield us right now. But doing this exhausts her so we don't have much time."

"Dad," she said. "Is Raffe looking for me?"

He forced a grim smile. "No, dear. He is looking for Bina and me."

"But why, Dad? I don't understand." She felt Harry's fingers tighten around her hand.

"Cristal," Harry said. "I'll explain later. Your dad has something to tell us and time is running out."

Her heart was beating hard against her ribs. Logic was what she needed at that moment but, considering the circumstances, nothing seemed very logical anymore.

"Harry's right. What do you need to tell us?" she said in a soft tone.

Her dad nodded his head. "Dark angels are using GN to continue the experiments of separating souls."

Harry said, "Separating souls?"

"GN have been doing experiments with parents of special gifted children. They kidnapped us to try to separate our souls."

Cristal interrupted. "Dad, why would they want to do that?"

"Demons are running the show at Global Nation. They wanted to extract our souls—for what exactly I don't know. My guess is that they were testing to see if they could implant the souls into their soulless bodies. They must have believed that they had to keep our physical bodies alive for the experiment to succeed. What they didn't expect was that Bina and I would escape from the labs and cross over to Limbo."

Cristal shivered. "I still don't understand what the big deal about souls is. And when you say "crossed over", is that another way of saying "dead"?" She held her breath as the tears burned her eyes.

"Darling," her dad said. "Demons want our souls and angels are tired of saving us from ourselves. Both sides are against us.

There is no good angel or bad angel. Remember that. Bina and I will contact you soon."

Cristal swallowed hard, half understanding what was being said but at the same time not wanting to hear any of it.

"Cristal, you have to be strong. I love you," he said.

The image of her father blurred in and out of focus then vanished.

PART II
GAME PLAN

In anguish, did I scream at the moon, the stars
while galaxies blazed
Each curdling cry
piercing all sound barriers and racing
the space that swallows...
the haunting images of the night
Take me away

AR Vasquez

CHAPTER 14
SOULS

Cristal had been lying on the couch for hours. Sleep evaded her even though every cell in her body begged to drift into a blissful stupor. But how could she sleep? Her father's words played back in her head like a broken record.

What did *souls* have to do with all of this? She wished she had paid more attention in her Catechism religion classes her parents had made her attend when she was a child.

She glanced over at Harry who was asleep, half sitting, and half slouching on the chair. Serena was sleeping on top of a blanket, which she had spread out on the floor. Gabriel was in his room, pleased to lie down in his own bed.

It seemed everyone but she had managed to fall asleep. She turned on her side, bending her legs and twisting to find a comfortable position. She closed her eyes and began breathing in deeply. Breathe in. Breathe out. After several deep breaths, she began to feel lightheaded. She welcomed the dizzying sensation, hoping it was bringing her closer to a deep slumber. The kind of sleep where you pass out into complete blackness and think of absolutely nothing until the blaring wail of the alarm jolts you wide awake.

A warm gust of air was brushing against her body, soothing her as she eased into a state of relaxation. *Almost there.* Pure physical exhaustion mixed with the euphoric feeling of drifting into a dreamless sleep overtook her senses.

Enjoy this slice of peace while you can.

WARM CARESSES AGAINST HER CHEEK. HER EYES WERE HEAVY as if she'd been drugged with sleeping pills, making them difficult, almost impossible to open. The caresses travelled down her arms. Gentle, soothing. Her body felt like it was being wrapped with a feather down quilt reminding her of the one she had when she was a little girl. The blanket was what comforted her after her dad had disappeared. It had helped her fall asleep then...

"Like it is helping you fall asleep now."

Her eyes flickered open.

"Kerim?" She squinted into the darkness, making out his face. She reached out in front of her. Was this all in her head?

"Cristal." His voice entered her mind.

Flashes of memory flooded her head. She remembered clearly how Kerim had tried to kill her with his sword. *Push him away. Get out of my head!*

"I came here to explain," his voice said.

"There's no need to explain."

She felt his fingers twisting and untwisting a strand of her hair the way he used to – when he was just a guy, her guy. She missed his touch, her cheek turning towards the warmth of his hand.

"Cristal," he whispered.

"Stop," she said, moving to push him away. *This is so wrong.* No matter how hard she wanted him to leave, her body betrayed her desires.

"Raffe and his army are still after me." His lips grazed her forehead.

Her lips parted. "So what do you want from me?" she said in a breathy voice. "Are you here to finish the job?"

A cold blast of air replaced the warmth of his hand on her cheek.

"Kerim?" she started to say. But she knew he was already gone.

CRISTAL SAT UPRIGHT AND PEERED INTO THE DARKNESS. THE sound of her heartbeat pounded loudly in her head.

On the ground, Serena mumbled something in her sleep and rolled onto her side.

Harry was sprawled over the chair, breathing deeply in between snores.

It seemed that no one else had noticed Kerim's unannounced visit. She lay back placing her hands behind her head and stared at the ceiling. Exhaustion was wrapping its arms around her and holding her down. She welcomed the sleep, longing for it. But just as much as she wanted to sleep, the ugly shackles of fear were preventing her from it. What if she fell asleep and never woke up again?

"CRISTAL," HARRY SAID IN HER EAR.

She turned away from him, her body aching to fall back into the drunkenness of uninterrupted slumber.

"We have to go."

She felt a hand on her shoulder.

"Harry, can't we give her a few more minutes?" she heard Serena say. "I think she had trouble sleeping last night."

Cristal forced one eye open. Sunlight was peeking through the window blinds, casting long shadows against the wall. Harry and Serena were still talking to each other. Dust particles danced in front of their faces like tiny snowflakes. They seemed unaware that she had awakened.

"I'm so tired," she said, the words barely scraping past her throat.

Serena turned and kneeled down beside her. "Get some rest. Harry can go to GN on his own."

Relieved to hear this, she closed her eye.

The gentle lulling of sleep was interrupted by shuffling sounds and hushed whispers. *Great.*

Gabriel's voice cut through the muffled conversation.

"I'm going with you Harry whether you want me to or not," he said.

The thought of Gabriel venturing out into the land of the living without her to protect him was a risk she wasn't prepared for him to take. "No, I want to go." She struggled to get up.

"Let me help you." She felt Harry's hand on her elbow.

The kind gesture was comforting in an odd way. Harry was the closest thing to family she had since her mother fell head over heels with her stepfather, the obnoxious dentist.

"Here," Harry said, reaching out his hand.

She paused a second before putting her hand in his. Harry's

fingers gently wrapped around hers. Their eyes met briefly and for a moment she sensed a longing in his gaze.

Serena coughed into her hand. "Okay, you two. Let's get to business. Or do you want Gabriel and I to leave the room?"

"Don't start any rumors," Harry said. He put his arm around Cristal's waist, helping her to her feet.

As she steadied herself, things around her shifted and the floor beneath her began to sway. *Oh no, not again.* She grabbed hold of Harry's jacket, anything to keep herself from teetering forward.

Gabriel appeared by her side. "Let me help."

In that moment, a high-pitched sound blasted into the room sending massive vibrations towards her. She let go of Harry to cover her ears. Losing her balance, she fell forward, landing into his arms.

"Are you okay?" he said, looking down at her.

"Can't you hear that horrible sound?" She was still pressing her hands over her ears.

"I don't hear anything. Where do you hear it?"

"From over there," she said, waving towards the window in the direction where the sound seemed to be coming from.

Gabriel slowly walked to the window as if an invisible force drew him to it. "I do hear it."

Cristal's eardrums were being pummeled by the unexplainable throbbing.

"I can hear it. It sounds so beautiful," Gabriel said. He was by the window now, reaching out to peek through the blinds. The light shone through from between the slats, cutting through Gabriel's chest and pouring out from his back onto the carpet.

"Gabriel," she said. She turned towards Harry and Serena to see their bewildered expressions on their faces.

He turned towards her and smiled. He looked so radiant and peaceful.

"I can't see him. Can you?" Serena whispered.

"No," Harry said. He took a step towards the window.

"Wait," Cristal said.

Gabriel was transforming. His physical self was softening around the edges as a haloed glow surrounded him giving off a bright heavenly lustrous light.

"The sound seems to be gone now," Gabriel said, oblivious to what was happening to him.

She realized that he was right. The high-pitched sound had disappeared the moment Gabriel began transforming.

"Cristal, you can see him?" Harry said in a low whisper.

"What's going on? Why are you whispering?" Gabriel asked. He frowned, a look of panic flashed across his face.

Cristal turned to Serena and Harry, her chest heavy with a sudden sadness.

"Cristal, what's going on?" Gabriel said, his voice going up a pitch.

"Look at yourself. Something is happening to you," she said. Her body was trembling and the last ounce of energy she had left was escaping from her.

"What do you mean?" he said. He glanced down and lifted his hand up to his face. Bright rays of light fanned out from the tips of his fingers up to the ceiling.

Cristal paused for a moment, trying to regain her balance. Something strange was happening to her too. She didn't know what it was but somehow she felt that whatever Gabriel was experiencing, for some crazy reason, she was experiencing it too.

CHAPTER 15
TREADING IN NEW TERRITORY

The plan for this morning was straightforward. Get to GN University to debrief Joanna about the events that happened in New York after the earthquake. Crossing back to this side should have meant that he could get back to the certainty of his life. But Gabriel disappearing into thin air and watching Cristal fade in and out meant that even on this side, things would never be the same again.

"Harry, don't just stand there. Grab Cristal's hand," Serena said. "Before she disappears too!"

She was right. There was no time to be philosophical about the situation.

Harry reached out and grabbed Cristal's hand. A jolt of energy surged from hers to his and up his arm into his body. The room began swelling around him. He glanced down noticing a rusty yellow glow emitting from his body.

"Harry," Cristal said, "They're saying that it's Gabriel's time to go." She turned and pointed towards the window.

He could see Gabriel or bits of him in between the rays of light that were shining through his body. His expression was the closest thing to what Harry could describe as euphoric. Gabriel had returned to the land of the living despite the warnings. He wasn't so sure what kind of angels were here to claim his soul and exactly where they were planning on taking him.

"Serena, find a string, anything you can tie around your wrist," Harry said. He had an idea that might work.

"Will do," she said, before disappearing into the kitchen.

Harry turned back to Cristal tightening his fingers around hers. "Try to focus on Gabriel. We won't let them take him away."

Cristal nodded her head and closed her eyes. She directed her words towards Gabriel's direction. "Gabriel, don't let them take you. It's not time yet. We need you here."

A look of confusion crossed Gabriel's face. He tilted his head as if someone else was speaking.

"Gabriel!" Harry said. "Don't trust them. It's not your time yet. Tell them to leave you alone. They cannot take you if you don't give them permission to do so."

Gabriel frowned. "Harry? Is that true?"

"Yes! Tell them to leave you alone."

Cristal joined in. "Tell them that you don't want to go!"

Serena was back holding up her wrist, which was sporting a string of beads. "I cut a piece of Gabriel's beaded curtains."

Gabriel's seventies fashion style was proving to be useful.

"Great. Grab Cristal's other hand."

Cristal stretched out her hand towards Serena who grabbed it. Serena's body trembled as the energy rushed through her body. The orange beads on her homemade bracelet began glowing.

Serena said, "We need to get Gabriel and form a circle around him."

What a brilliant idea. "You're right," he said. "Let's go."

"Hold on tight," Cristal said. She took a step forward, her arms pulled back. Using all her power, she pulled Harry and Serena forward, launching them in the air. The motion catapulted them towards Gabriel.

They were flying at super high speed but time appeared to be suspended, at least from Harry's perspective. Everything around him seemed to be moving in slow motion. It was surreal to see Serena with a fiery look of determination on her face and her right arm positioned—a super hero in flight. What was even more bizarre was Cristal who was unrecognizable—her body had transformed into a white blaze of furious energy.

Gabriel was frantically waving, but the motion was slowed down at ninety frames a second making it almost comical to watch.

Serena's voice snapped Harry back into real time.

"Gabriel! Grab my hand now!" Serena cried out.

Something was blocking them from reaching Gabriel. They hovered in front of him, in skydiving position, head up, arms and legs spread open.

GABRIEL WAS BLUBBERING LIKE A BABY. "IT'S NOT MY TIME. I want to stay here. I don't want to go with them!"

"Focus on us! Can you grab our hands?" Harry said.

What sounded like thunder erupted above them. But could thunder vocalize commands?

"Your time has come." The words from the thunderous being were wrapped around the roar of the wind.

Harry felt an electric shock go through him. White streaks of energy ran from his right arm where he was holding Cristal's hand through his body and out from his other hand. He pointed it towards the invisible shield in front of them. He looked over at Serena who was doing the same thing. Now this was cool.

Each blast brought them closer to Gabriel by a magnetic force.

"Grab their hands, Gabriel!" Cristal said, her voice sounding more like a lion roar.

Gabriel reached out again, his fingers barely touching Serena's. "I can't seem to!"

He reached out for the third time managing to reach her hand, the tips of his fingers sliding through.

Serena turned to them. "It's not working. He's not in a physical state."

"I've got to do this myself," Cristal said. She released them from her grip.

What was she doing?

With Harry and Serena not tapping into her energy, Cristal seemed to swell to four times her size while transforming into a giant orb of white light.

Harry and Serena were still suspended in the air, hovering a few feet away from Cristal as she took over the show.

"Hold my hand," she said, her voice as deafening as thunder. She raised her right arm, the charm bracelet emitting blue rays of light as she turned towards something that he couldn't see. "I order you to leave Gabriel!"

Harry held his breath. He still couldn't believe that Cristal was no longer the timid, unsure girl he had once known.

"Go Cristal, get him," Serena said beneath her breath.

"Child, do you know who you speak with?" the invisible being asked.

Cristal had her arm around Gabriel, protecting him with the force shield she was forming around them.

"I don't give a crap who you are. You heard what I said. I command you to leave."

"Yeah!" Gabriel piped in. "Leave me alone!"

The building began shaking around them. The wind howled—a wolf calling its pack.

"In the name of God, the Father Almighty, creator of Heaven and Earth, leave now!" Cristal cried out.

A deathly silence swallowed the sound of the howling wind. And where Cristal and Gabriel had stood was now a gaping black hole.

CHAPTER 16
REALITY HITS HARD

Serena grabbed Harry's forearm before he could take another step toward the hole.

"Not a good idea," she said.

The hole constricted and closed shut.

He shook his arm from Serena's grip. "Why did you do that? We can't just let them disappear!"

Serena grabbed a backpack from the couch and ran to the front door. "Having you disappear with them isn't going to help anyone." She stopped and turned back. "Well, are you coming?"

Harry knew she was right. Serena was the only one thinking with her head and not her emotions right now so he resigned himself to let her take the lead.

"Yeah, of course." He came up beside her. "Glad you thought of packing supplies."

"And weapons," she said, opening the door and peeking outside. She turned back and gave a quick nod to indicate the coast was clear. She waved with her two fingers to follow her as she stepped into the hallway.

Harry looked around and grabbed Gabriel's 12-inch black aluminum flashlight on the side table. That could come in handy later.

The hallway was dark except for the light that was coming in from the window at the other end of the building. Serena picked up her pace, waving for him to do the same. He jogged up and ran alongside her until they reached the elevator.

"Let's take the stairs," he said, taking back the lead.

"Roger that," she said.

Harry opened the door to the stairwell with Serena two steps behind. The darkness was banished as he flicked on the flashlight. They rushed down the stairs, the "thud" sound of their shoes echoing around them as they ran.

"This is the lobby," Serena said once they reached the bottom landing.

She pulled open the door and peeked out. She motioned with her fingers to follow and stepped out with him right behind her.

The lobby was as he had remembered it the last time he had seen Gabriel, except for the fact that it was dark. Serena was already rushing towards the exit, pushing the glass door open. He stepped outside as she let the door swing close behind them.

The devastation at street level was more graphic than from what they had seen from Gabriel's apartment. If an earthquake had not hit the city, the bodies lying on the sidewalk might have been mistaken for sleeping homeless people. The sight of an arm, a leg and other body parts peeking out from under the rubble and debris made his gut hurt.

He turned to Serena puzzled about the situation. "I don't

understand why or how the bodies are still intact? The earth-quake happened months ago," he said.

"What bodies?"

He turned back, waving his hand to show her.

"Sorry, Harry. I don't see any bodies."

"What do you mean you can't see any..."

His mouth fell open. She was right. There were no signs of bodies in sight. Had he been imagining things?

"Oh my God," he heard Serena say.

He turned and saw that she was facing back towards Gabriel's building. Her face was pale almost as if she'd seen a ghost. His gaze followed hers. He sucked in his breath when reality sunk in.

Gabriel's building was nothing more than a pile of charred rubble.

CHAPTER 17
DESCENT

The building shook from side to side while the wind roared around them. Cristal searched her childhood memories of her weekly religion classes. Did the nuns teach her anything she could use right now? She vaguely remembered Sister Theresa telling them about asking the Holy Spirit for divine intervention. Question was, how? She had no clue. All she could muster was a snippet from the Apostle's creed prayer, which wasn't much but it was better than nothing.

"In the name of God, the Father Almighty, creator of Heaven and Earth, leave now!" she cried out.

She bit her lip in anticipation, praying that it would work.

Powerful waves of energy started closing in on them and the floor beneath her began giving way.

Here we go.

She locked her arm into Gabriel's.

"Hold on," she said, as the blackness swallowed them whole.

ALTHOUGH IT SEEMED LIKE HOURS OF FREE FALLING IN PITCH-black nothingness, she realized that in this space, wherever it was, there was no real sense of time. Well at least not the way she understood time.

How could they even tell if they were going downward, not upwards or sideways? There were no walls or structures around them to distinguish what was up or down. No air. No wind. No motion. It was a vast emptiness.

And yet, she sensed something. She felt it in her bones. In this real life horror movie, someone or something had slashed the cables to this elevator ride to Hell. Her stomach flopped at the thought.

"What's happening to us?" Gabriel asked.

All she could say was, "We have to get out of here."

"What about the bracelet?" Gabriel said. "You can teleport us out, right?"

"Right. It got us to New York, so it should get us back there." She was putting the plan together in her head when a surge of heat rose up and wrapped its arms around her. She lifted her wrist to check the bracelet; sweat pouring from her armpits.

Gabriel said, "Man, it feels like a bloody oven in here."

"Yeah, I'm melting into a puddle of sweat. We really have to find a way out."

"So what's taking you so long?"

"I don't know but you squawking at me isn't helping matters." She shook her wrist expecting to see the bracelet spring to life. It hung like the inert object it was—just a piece of *girly* jewelry. "I wish this thing came with instructions," she said, fumbling with the globe charm.

"Let me see that," Gabriel said, reaching out to touch it. "Maybe you have to say something."

She could barely keep herself together. The bracelet was fading in and out of focus and her lungs were tightening as if they were filling up with smoke. And to top it off, the scorching heat was burning through her shoes, licking the bottoms of her feet.

What *if* this was the end for both of them? What if they were both falling into the fires of Hell?

Her pulse was racing, her head spiraling into dizzying circles. No, no, no!

"Hey, Cristal, are you even trying?"

"Something is happening again. I think I'm going to pass out." She could hear the panic in her own voice.

"You have to be kidding, right?" Gabriel grabbed her by the arm. His eyes were as wide as saucers. "Get a grip on yourself! You're the only one who can get us out of here!"

He was right. She needed to focus. Breathe.

She grabbed the globe charm and pushed all her will towards it. "Destination: Global Nation."

Nothing. The invisible flames were doing a tango around her, whipping her exposed skin at every spin.

Gabriel squeezed her arm harder, raising his voice as he spoke. "Maybe you have to pray or something."

"What makes you think I know how to do that?"

"Well, you're the one who went to Sunday school. And you're the one with special powers!"

"Yelling at me isn't helping, okay?" she snapped.

Gabriel's mouth dropped open, a look of hurt flashing across his face.

She tried to soften her tone. "And it wasn't Sunday school. They were on Thursday nights."

It seemed stupid to be arguing about such a silly fact but it was her only way to keep sane with all the madness around her. Gabriel *did* have a point and she needed to focus on it.

Was there something she learned in Catechism classes that she could use here?

Dear God, help me, please.

The bracelet began vibrating, the tiny globe spinning like a top. The breeze generated from the spinning globe was a sweet relief as it pushed the heat wave away.

"Cristal, it's working," Gabriel said, releasing his grip on her arm.

"I think I figured how it works," she said. "Hold on."

CHAPTER 18
ASK, SEEK, KNOCK

She closed her eyes, letting the bits of her childhood memories flood into her head. A flash of scenes from her life popped up in her head like someone was flipping the channels with the TV remote, finally stopping on one scene.

She recalled something she learned in Catechism religion classes about the Gospel of Matthew.

Sister Theresa's words replayed in her mind, "Ask and it shall be given you; seek, and you shall find; knock, and it shall be opened unto you."

Somehow, the memory flashback had to be a clue of some sort. Why else would she be remembering this now while plunging towards an unforeseen death?

A voice in her head whispered, *Ask*.

Okay, doesn't hurt to give it a shot.

She looked upward and said, "Dear God, are You there? It's me, Cristal."

The globe charm started emitting a soft white light.

Gabriel nodded his head, and pleaded with his eyes for her to continue.

The voice whispered, *Seek.*

Okay, it couldn't hurt to try. "How do we find our way out from here, dear Lord?"

The globe swelled to double its size.

"Keep going," Gabriel said. "If we can get to GN, we can find Harry and Serena."

"Okay, let me concentrate." Cristal reached out and touched the surface of the globe. An electric shock ran up her hand but unlike the first time, instead of a map peeling off and magnifying in front of her, the globe continued spinning.

Gabriel frowned. "Why isn't it working?"

Sometimes the answer to a problem is so simple that you don't see it, she remembered telling Harry. And yet now even with the clues, she couldn't figure out what the answer was. Unless it really was that simple.

She closed her fist and reached out to the globe again, knocking three times.

CHAPTER 19
EXPECT THE UNEXPECTED

The sharp smell of fresh coffee brought Cristal to her senses. Her eyelids were heavy, her head balancing on her neck like a bowling ball on a pin.

"Welcome," a deep guttural sounding voice said.

Cristal forced her eyes open, wincing from the rays of sunlight flooding the room.

"Where am I?" she said, the words were like cotton in her mouth. She struggled to sit up despite every muscle in her body begging her not to. She tried to establish her surroundings but the glare of the sun blinded her eyes.

"You are in safe house," said the male voice. The strong Hebrew accent and the strange way he spoke seemed so uncomfortably familiar. She wished she could shake the fog out of her head so that she could put two and two together.

"Safe house," she repeated to herself.

Her eyes were adjusting to the light now and she could make out three single beds in the room, she being in one of them.

Hanging on the far wall were pictures of three school age girls standing with a young man. They all had dark wavy hair, olive colored complexions and large toothy grins. She recognized them right away having seen these pictures every day when she shared the bedroom with Walid's sisters.

Her nose caught the welcoming smell of fresh bread baking in the oven. After everything she'd been through in the last few weeks, she realized how much she missed the little things like waking up to that sweet aroma every morning.

"Welcome back."

Her gaze quickly shifted to the darker corner of the room. Leaning on the edge of the desk was Archangel Rafael, his stocky tanned arms crossed over a snug white t-shirt revealing his muscular chest.

"Do not fear, girl," he said.

"Girl?" She snorted back a laugh, unsure if her reaction was one of fear or just general hysteria.

"Do you prefer "Boy"?" he said with a scornful tone as he sauntered toward her. He seemed to be flexing the muscles in his legs and arms on purpose, as if to remind her of his power.

Don't show your fear. "I prefer you call me by my given name," she said, her voice soft but steady.

Raffe's lips curled into a half smile. "Very well, then, Cristal. And you can call me Raffe when I am in my human form."

"Raffe works for me." Her casual retort masked the frantic thoughts in her mind. *How fast can he switch to his angel form?* Would she be able to summon her powers to defend herself in time? Worse yet, could he hear her thoughts?

He tilted his head, his stare panning down her body. Did angels have X-ray vision? She gagged at the thought.

"Why don't you take a picture? It'll last longer, you pervert," she said, pulling the sheet up to her neck.

A scowl crossed his face while his glare locked into hers. "I have no need for carnal pleasures that the male species of your human race find so alluring. I'm merely ensuring that you are not hiding a weapon," he growled.

"Weapon?" Her eyes narrowed as her instincts played out different ways to counter should Raffe make an offensive move.

"As I say earlier, you are in safe house. You need not fear me here."

Back at Gabriel's apartment Harry had mentioned something about the place where both worlds overlapped. And didn't he send her the same message via morse code right before Kerim tried to attack her with a sword? Was it possible that where the worlds overlapped, angels couldn't hurt humans? Was that what Raffe meant when he called this place a safe house?

"I don't fear you here. Or anywhere to that matter," she said.

He smiled, his broad face widening further exposing his popcorn colored teeth. "Your humor refreshes me. You are very much like Liora, the mother of your father's mother. I forgot how she could make me laugh." He leaned his head back, opened his mouth and chortled as if to prove his point.

"Where is Gabriel?" she asked, hoping this would focus the conversation back to the present.

His smile dissolved into a sneer. "This is what I want to ask you."

"I just woke up from a ride to Hell's kitchen. How would I know where he is?"

"That's a fair comment."

"Fair? Nothing about this is fair. If you're talking about fairness, tell me what you want from Gabriel."

"Silly mortal," he said, chuckling to himself.

The veins in her temples felt like they were going to explode.

Keep calm. He'll give you the answers you need if you remain calm, a voice said in her head.

Dad, are you sure?

CHAPTER 20
TRUCE OR DARE

R affe yawned into his hand. After a few seconds of silence, he focused his dark ink-filled eyes at her. "It is my mission to bring him to where he should be."

Keep calm. "And where exactly is that?"

"Purgatory," he said in a matter-of-fact tone.

Her heart began pounding in her chest. "I don't understand."

"Your friend was foolish to return to the land of the living is violation of Divine Law. This matter, along with your father's bad behavior in Limbo, was flagged as Level Two escalation."

"My father? And sorry, what exactly is Level Two escalation?"

Raffe sighed. "It means Divine Heads are extremely, how as you Americans say, 'ticked off' about this. Gabriel's actions, your father and Harry's mother, set very dangerous precedent." He paused for dramatic effect. "A precedent that undermine co-existence of all realms, Heaven, Earth and Hell."

She gave him a blank stare.

He sighed the way her stepfather would when he was not in the mood to be bothered.

"When a mortal dies and his soul cross over to Holy side, demons can no longer claim the mortal soul. In this case, your father and mother of Harry are resisting summons to enter Purgatory. Gabriel left safety of Limbo by his own will, opening door for demons to take his soul.

Never in history has a soul admitted to realm of Limbo crossed back to land of living. If demons succeed in capturing Gabriel's soul, it will be big disgrace for the Divine Heads. A disgrace that starts war to end all wars."

She shuddered but tried to remain composed. "You tried to kill me. Why should I trust you?"

Raffe's smirk acknowledged the hypocrisy of the situation. "The Commander-in-Chief believes that, for now, you are more useful in land of the living than in spiritual realm."

Cristal swung her legs off the side of the bed and faced him. "What exactly does useful mean? I thought that God was afraid that I'd open the portal for demons to enter Limbo. Wasn't that why you were sent to kill me in the first place?"

"This is not for you to question. Do not challenge His orders. "

"So just to clarify. The order to kill me has been cancelled?"

"Actually, my new assignment is to be your guardian. Call it a truce for now," he said with a half smile.

"My guardian."

"Yes."

"And Kerim?"

"Ahh, yes, Kerim." He glanced towards the window, staring off into the distance as he spoke. "Kerim has made grave choice to fall from our Father's grace. He no longer is part of my Holy Army. Very unfortunate."

A soft knock on the door interrupted their discussion.

"Mizz Cristal." The sound of Walid's voice came through the door. "Will you be joining us for the morning meal?"

Raffe lifted his chin giving her the signal to respond.

"Yes, Walid," she said. "I'll be joining you."

"Do you want Nazreen to help?"

Raffe shook his head, signaling her to decline.

"No, I'll be fine. Thank you," she said.

"Okay, glad that you are feeling better. We will wait for you at the table then."

Raffe waited for the footsteps to move away before he turned to her.

"I must leave now," he said.

Cristal stood up. "Wait. What about Gabriel?"

"Not your worry. Focus on your own mission."

"Mission? What do you mean?"

He threw her a smirk. "You will know in time. If the Commander-in-Chief believes in you, so you must believe in yourself."

"But..."

"I must go. I sense Gabriel is in a bit of hot sauce and needs my help." He threw his head back and cackled.

He still thinks he's a comedian.

Before she could respond, Raffe walked past her, slid open the window and climbed out.

PART III
RESIST

Forgiveness: another feather to fall from wing
    Strip away this shallowness her dying heart shrieks
    Let me see, let me feel, let me hear you care, let me see you care, let me
feel you care
    Don't leave me here
    in this degrading cell.

AR Vasquez

CHAPTER 21
WHERE BOTH WORLDS OVERLAP, NEW YORK

Serena was white as a ghost. She stared in the direction where a disaster zone had replaced Gabriel's building. It all seemed so crazy because they had just exited from the building moments earlier. Serena was quick on her feet. She ran back towards the rubble, lifting her wrist to hold up the homemade orange beaded bracelet in front of her like a shield.

"I'll be right back," she called out, stepping into where the apartment's entrance had been.

"What are you talking about?" he said.

She vanished into thin air only to return moments later with a smile as wide as a slice of watermelon.

"This is incredible," she said.

"Are you confirming what I'm thinking?" It didn't take him long to absorb what had just happened. In this world, Gabriel's building no longer existed. But because his building was the place where both worlds crossed, Harry and Serena were able to cross over and enter the building. This would be their safe house.

"Eyes might be on us. We need to be on the Q.T.," she said, pulling her hoodie over her head.

"Roger that." Q.T., or being on the quiet, made sense. No telling who or what was out there waiting to find the portal.

No time to lose. They had to reach GN to gather intel and assess the situation.

He followed Serena as she ran ahead, weaving in and out of obstructions on the sidewalk. The streets were eerily empty, except for the occasional man or woman searching through the rubble. Searching for food, or maybe a missing loved one?

Harry had to push the unnerving thoughts from his mind and focus on the mission at hand. Despite his bravado, his gut wrenched at the desolation and damage the earthquake had brought onto what used to be a vibrant and bustling city.

Focus on the mission.

From his quick assessment, he concluded that Gabriel's street had received the worst damage from the quake. Buildings were still standing, but there was evidence of excessive fire and water damage to most of the private residences and commercial establishments in the city. Giant swollen cracks in the sidewalks and the streets made what should have been an easy fifteen-minute jog stretch out to a forty-five minute obstacle course. Joanna's text message to Cristal had been dead on—New York City had become a war zone.

A group of men stepped in front of them as they reached the GN campus, appearing out of nowhere. At a glance, they could have easily passed for homeless people, their clothes ripped and hanging from their wafer thin bodies. He counted five men, although it was possible that there were more hidden nearby. Harry could only guess that they had been hiding in the shadows, watching them coming. Two of the men couldn't have been any older than Harry himself. The other three were maybe in their late thirties or early forties.

The tallest one, presumably the leader, lifted up a wooden baseball bat and pointed it at Harry.

"Where you two running off to?" he asked with a snarl.

Serena gave Harry a side-glance. He closed his fist, signaling for her to stand down.

"We don't want any trouble," Harry said calmly.

"What's in the backpack?" The man stepped toward Serena.

"My gear," she said, not batting an eye.

"Oh yeah? Hand it over." He waved the bat at her.

The other men began circling around them. From the hungry look in their eyes, he presumed that they hadn't eaten a real meal in weeks.

"Listen guys. We work for Global Nation. Let us go and we can see if we can get some food for you," Harry said.

The tall man whirled around and pointed the bat at him.

"You work for Global Nation? You think that means anything to us? After the quake, you GN jerks took over every major city in America. You froze our money in the banks, took our homes and slammed a curfew on us. GN stripped us of our rights and forced ordinary trusting citizens to comply with the new mandatory RF chip implant program."

Harry and Serena exchanged glances.

"Oh yes, your marketing team promoted the program with their billion dollar slick corporate style campaign as if they were selling the cure to cancer. They promised that the RF chips would ensure every American would have shelter, food, supplies and medical care.

"But in exchange for this, only people who got the implants were included in the 'all-American-GN-Will-Save-You' program.

It's corporate blackmail no matter how the marketing geeks and politicians want to spin it. And curse you! I will starve before I let you number me like cattle, you apocalyptic demons."

The other men joined him in the verbal attack and yelled obscenities in agreement, chanting, "Death to Global Nation!"

Harry was about to give Serena the signal to run when a military green Humvee drove up alongside them.

A monotone voice blasted from a speaker attached to the top of the vehicle. "This is a curfew zone. You are in violation of sections 452 and 275 of the curfew law; loitering or gathering of more than two individuals in a public place. You are all ordered to disperse immediately."

The leader of the group eyed the military vehicle with caution.

"I repeat, this is a curfew zone. Disperse immediately or we will arrest you."

It was obvious that the odds of them succeeding were low. Come on. A wooden bat against automatic firearms? The man lowered his bat and nodded to the others. They scattered in different directions, leaving Harry and Serena to face the soldiers on their own.

Serena gave him a "What now?" look. With a quick hand signal, he told her to remain still.

The passenger side door swung open and a tall man wearing dark sunglasses and a brown leather jacket stepped out of the vehicle onto the sidewalk in front of them. Harry noted the outline of the holster, which was hidden snug against the inside of his jacket. This guy wasn't Army or NYPD.

"Global Nation Security," he said as if to answer his thoughts. "Your papers, please."

Harry tilted his head, his eyes narrowing. "Kerim?"

CHAPTER 22
GLOBAL NATION

If Kerim was trying to intimidate them, he didn't know who he was up against. At least that's what Harry thought.

"You know who I am," Harry said.

Kerim repeated in a cold tone. "Your papers now or I'll be forced to arrest you."

Serena stepped forward, her hands clenched. "Don't act like you don't know us. Do your goons know what you really are?"

Kerim lifted his hand and shot a bolt of energy at her chest. She dodged the blast by diving right, landing on the ground and letting her right shoulder absorb the impact.

"That was just a warning," Kerim said, before turning back to Harry.

Serena sprung to her feet, raising her fists in front of her, ready to attack.

"Stand down, Serena," Harry said. The last thing he needed was for Kerim to send a blast at them with full intent to injure.

Serena eyed Kerim, her fury simmering to medium. "Roger that."

Harry could feel Kerim's stone cold glare burn through his dark shades.

"Papers, now."

"Okay," he said, reaching into his jacket pocket.

"Slowly. And keep the other hand up where I can see it," Kerim said.

"Yeah, okay. Don't worry; I am not going to shoot you with my passport," he said, handing it to him.

"Now yours," Kerim said, turning to Serena.

She shot Harry a burning glance, reached into her pocket and pulled out her passport.

"Why do we have to show you our passports? You know who we are," she said.

"Our scans show that you both don't have the required RF identification chips implants. Without it, GN requires proof of identity."

"Guess, treating your friends like criminals is how angels roll these days?" she said, sarcasm seeping into her words as she handed her passport to him.

Kerim flipped through the passports, ignoring her comment.

"Do you have a valid US Visa, Ms. Keensley?"

Serena's eyes widened. "It's Keensky. And what do you mean visa? You know how we got here."

Kerim waved his hand and two soldiers jumped out of the backseat of the Humvee.

"Put Ms. Keensky in the back," he ordered.

"Yes, sir!" The first soldier grabbed Serena by the arm.

"Let me go!" She struggled to free herself from the soldier's grip.

"What the hell is going on, Kerim?" Harry said, rushing up to the soldier.

Kerim nodded for the soldier to move aside.

"Ms. Keensky is on American soil illegally. We are detaining her for questioning."

Harry glanced at Serena before turning back to Kerim. "She's my wife and as an American citizen, she has every right to be here."

Kerim tilted his head. "Wife? Perhaps you can show me the marriage certificate."

Serena interrupted. "We were married on the day of the quake."

Kerim turned to Harry. "When and where did you get married?"

Harry didn't flinch. "In Cyprus, the day of the quake." He knew that Israel didn't recognize civil or non-religious marriages. It was popular for non-religious Israelis to fly to Cyprus for a quick wedding.

Kerim turned to Serena. "Cyprus. And who witnessed the wedding?"

She raised her chin. "Gabriel Windham."

CHAPTER 23

LIONHEART

Her presence was as daunting as it was the first time Harry had met her. Shelley Lionheart, director and president of Global Nation sat with her back straight in her white leather executive chair, a menacing leader who loved to flaunt it. From her blue black raven colored hair cropped close to her scalp to the long manicured nails painted a bold blood red, matching the color of her thick lips.

Dressed in a tailored white dress suit, her coffee colored skin tone made for a dramatic contrast, masking her underlying cold-blooded thoughts. If anyone asked Harry, he'd describe her as a boa constrictor with very expensive taste.

Her amber colored eyes bore into his brain, drilling for information. "It's been a while since we've had a chance to chat. Hasn't it?"

Harry cleared his throat, shifting slightly in his seat. "Yes, Ms. Lionheart. The last time we met was the day you hired me."

She leaned back and flashed her unnaturally neon white teeth.

"Call me Shelley. We're all family here. No need for formalities."

She'd said the same thing the day she interviewed him.

"Yes, right. Of course, Shelley."

"The usual protocol is that your senior manager, George Beaver, be the one to debrief you after returning from assigned projects overseas. But I've specifically requested to debrief you myself."

From the corner of his eye, something moved. His ears picked up shuffling noises and voices. He had a sinking feeling that they were not alone.

Lionheart raised an eyebrow, noticing his unease.

"I am recording this conversation, in case you're wondering."

"Yes, sure." It didn't look like he had an option.

She folder her arms on the desk and leaned forward.

"We're giving you your own private room, Harry. It is quite a luxury considering we have so many people who are staying in shared quarters."

"Um. Thanks but that's not necessary."

"Don't look a gift horse in the mouth. Be flattered. Not everyone can enjoy their privacy these days."

"Thank you. When can I see my wife?"

She nodded her head. "Ah, yes. The wife. I need to ask you a few questions before we discuss the matter about your new bride."

He swallowed hard and gave her a polite smile. "No problem."

"Dr. Saeed Nariman. Tell me everything about what you know about his time at our Tel Aviv campus."

Harry hadn't expected the line of questioning to go in this

direction. "Well, Dr. Saeed arrived in Tel Aviv a few days after I did. He said he was working on GN sanctioned research."

Her eyebrows furrowed into a knot. "And what exactly did the research entail?"

"The time travel theory that he had been working on."

"You mean, the theory your father was working on," she said.

"Um, yes. That's right." Okay, where she was going with this and why?

"And how is Aaron, your father, doing these days?"

Harry's heart started racing. As far as the world knew, Aaron Doub was dead.

On the day of the earthquake Harry had witnessed with his own eyes his supposedly dead father, Aaron Doub, alive and well in Dr. Saeed's secret lab. At the time, part of him wondered if it was all a hallucination. But after all the supernatural events he'd witnessed since then, the reality of his father being alive wasn't far-fetched any more.

"Harry, do you have something you want to say?"

"As you know, my father died several years ago. I may have seen someone in Dr. Saeed's lab that reminded me of my father. But then again, I was running on very little sleep at the time and could have been imagining things."

"Hmm. Imagining things." She reached for her mouse and turned her monitor towards him.

She moved the mouse arrow over a video player on the screen and clicked play.

The video had the GN Tel Aviv Hebrew logo plastered in the right corner. In the video there were, guessing from their age and attire, a few students scrambling in the background while soldiers shoved other people to the side. Another soldier escorted a man in a lab coat towards the center of the screen. The man looked off to the side and then nodded his head as if he had been given a signal from someone behind the camera.

The man in the video was Dr. Saeed. No question about it. Harry leaned forward, curious to hear what he had to say.

"You are all aware that Israel is in a state of emergency. We know that the earthquake is a global event affecting major cities around the world.

"Jerusalem was one of the epicenters of the quake and was the hardest hit. The President, Prime Minister and cabinet members have officially been confirmed dead. The Knesset building in Givat Ram, Jerusalem was destroyed in the earthquake and all Knesset members are either confirmed dead or are missing.

"Global Nation is working with all countries to bring order to a world that is swirling with chaos. Today we are announcing that the State of Israel has appointed a new leader. This is to ensure the security and safety for the people and the state of Israel. On behalf of Global Nation Tel Aviv, I am proud to announce Aaron Doub as the new President of the State of Israel."

Harry almost fell out of his chair. In the video, his father Aaron was being escorted into the room. Dr. Saeed handed him a small card to read.

"You may all be wondering how I could be standing here now when I was declared deceased in 2008. I am living proof that my theory of time travel is no longer a theory. In the experiments that Dr. Saeed and I have worked on, I travelled from 2008 to 2013. As your new president, I will work closely with GN Tel Aviv to restore and improve civilization here in Israel and ensure that the state of Palestine will be realized.

We will continue our experiments in time travel to see what

our future holds for us and prevent anything that would or could harm our nation."

Harry sucked in his breath when Aaron looked straight into the camera. His father's eyes were glowing a fluorescent shade of yellow.

CHAPTER 24
INTERROGATION

Lionheart questioned him for an hour, trying to uncover any knowledge he had of Dr. Saeed's scheme or whom he was working for. She ended the interrogation after he repeatedly denied knowing anything.

Of course, he never mentioned the demon and angel battle that happened in Akko right before Cristal opened the portal to Limbo. "Don't ask, don't tell" was his motto.

"About the matter with your bride," she said. "Since Cyprus' City Hall was destroyed by the quake, we have no way of disproving your marriage."

He shifted uneasily in his seat. He had to play this one by instinct, knowing that Serena was being questioned in the other room.

"Which also means you have no way of proving it either." She leaned back in her chair, drumming her nails on the armrest. "No worries. We'll have a civil ceremony here at GN. I'm sure we can summon a Justice of the Peace for you."

"Okay..." he said. *What was she up to?*

Lionheart tapped a button on her desk phone.

"Beaver, go ahead with the preparations. Try to find musicians and anyone who can cook us a fancy meal. We're having a big wedding at GN in the rose garden. It's exactly what we need to bring up the morale around here."

Beaver's voice crackled on the speaker. "Yes, Shelley. Who will be attending?"

Lionheart waved her arm in the air. "Why everyone, of course!"

"Everyone?"

The smile on her face faded for a moment. "Isn't that what I just said?"

"But we have over thirty thousand people living on campus in the converted shelters and dorms."

"Figure it out Beaver." She punched a button to end the call.

She turned to Harry. "I'm assuming you don't have a thing to wear."

He frowned. "We really don't have to make this an extravagant affair."

She stood up and walked around her desk. "Don't be silly. The son of the President of Israel doesn't get married every day you know. Now stand up so that I can get my seamstress to measure you."

As if on cue, the door opened and a short pudgy lady holding a measuring tape and white seamstress chalk entered the office.

"I need you to whip up a sharp looking tuxedo for Mr. Doubt. After you're done, you'll be taking the measurements for his bride to be. Beaver has her in his office."

Upon hearing his name, Beaver poked his head into the room. "I have Harry's bride waiting in my office."

Lionheart gave him a curt nod. "I'll summon you once we're ready. And as you can see, we're not ready yet." She waved her hand to dismiss him.

What a dweeb.

Beaver shot Harry a dirty look before closing the door.

CHAPTER 25
HUSBAND AND WIFE

Lionheart pulled out all the stops. A makeshift orchestra made up of citizens who had indicated they could play an instrument accompanied the ceremony.

Harry had to admit he looked sharp in his tailored tuxedo. He had to do a double take when Serena walked down the aisle. It was the first time he'd seen her in anything that didn't resemble a tracksuit. She looked like a fairy maiden in her simple but elegant white gown, her dirty blonde hair swept up to the side, held by a jeweled barrette which Lionheart picked from her own jewelry collection—a wedding gift she'd said. The only other piece of jewelry she wore was the orange beaded bracelet. Despite looking like a princess, Serena seemed out of her comfort zone, blowing strands of stray hairs from the corner of her mouth and rolling her eyes when he tried to wink at her.

To Harry's surprise, the mayor of New York, Bill de Blasio, officiated the ceremony. Anyone watching from the wings might have wondered if Prince William was getting married here. Cameras were flashing at every moment like the paparazzi.

"By the powers vested in me by the City of New York and Global Nation, I now pronounce you husband and wife," the mayor said. "You may kiss the bride."

Harry gulped looking out at the sea of people watching. *I may kiss the bride?* Serena grabbed him by the collar and planted her lips on his. He swooned, not expecting her to do that.

The crowd erupted in cheers.

Lionheart was right. This wedding was definitely a boost to everyone's morale. Especially his.

❧

IT WAS BEYOND SURREAL. LIONHEART SAT AT THE HEAD TABLE in a neon white pantsuit that hugged her curvaceous body. In contrast, a blood red feather boa coiled around her neck. On her right sat Roshenbaum, the President of the United States of America with the First Lady, and on her left was the Mayor of New York and his wife. The President looked grim while he and Lionheart discussed stately matters. The Mayor and his wife, on the other hand, were sipping their glasses of champagne almost as if they thought it would be their last.

Harry gazed over at his new bride. The word "bride" sounded foreign yet appealing to his ears. But there she was sitting beside him, picking at her food while sneaking glances at him and trying very hard not to giggle. He found himself grinning when for what seemed the hundredth time the wedding guests tapped their glasses, egging them to kiss. The first few times he'd hesitated, not wanting to cross the line with Serena.

But between the sips of champagne and the sweet teasing

between Serena and himself, the magic of the evening dulled the anxiety that had been choking him the last few days.

"Kiss her!" Ting, ting, ting. *Here they go again.*

Closing his eyes and leaning forward until their lips pressed against each other seemed absolutely how it was meant to be. He had to admit that each kiss was more electrifying than the last.

All of his senses were focused on one thing—Serena's velvet soft lips melting into his. He could smell the subtle scent of coconut from her hair. The touch of her hand on his knee and the sweet taste of her lips made his head spin.

The sound of haunting piano chords cut through his thoughts.

"Oh, I love this song," she whispered into his mouth as their kiss ended.

Harry opened his eyes and was met by her dreamy stare. A deep sounding tenor voice began singing along with the piano— John Legend's "All of Me." Not one of his favorites, but it seemed to be growing on him.

She flashed him a pixie playful smile and winked. "Guess it's time for the bride and groom's first dance."

He could feel his cheeks burn. For whatever reason, Cristal's face flashed into his mind. He suddenly realized how stupid his decade long one-sided secret crush with Cristal actually was. A huge weight of self-inflicted romantic anguish seemed to lift off his shoulders.

Serena grabbed him by the arm and pulled him onto the dance floor.

"We have to convince everybody this is the real deal," she said as she hugged him close, pressing her body against his.

Multiple zones in his body were now mirroring the heat in his face.

"Who said this wasn't the real deal?" he whispered in her ear. He blinked hard, not believing what he'd just said.

"Why Harry, this is a side I never thought you had." She flashed him another smile, which lit up the room.

He looked over her shoulder, scanning the courtyard. The "guests" were smiling, dancing and clapping, as he'd expect to see at a wedding. Well, more like a macabre wedding of sorts, with the guests all dressed in grey GN jogging suits—Lionheart's solution for keeping the masses of people clothed or her way of marking them like the prisoners that they really were.

"What's wrong, Harry?"

"Look at everyone having a good time. It's hard to believe that outside the campus, the rest of the world is a disaster zone," he said.

"Maybe people need to forget the horror, even if it's just for a few hours," she said, her voice now soft and distant.

"Wish I could forget," he said, his voice softening like hers.

"You know what I wish? That you'd shut up and enjoy yourself for a change," she whispered into his ear.

A commotion by the gate interrupted their slow dance. Glancing up, they caught sight of Kerim and his men as they entered the courtyard. Kerim's hand was pulled up to the side of his face as he talked into his earpiece and headed straight towards them.

"Congratulations Mr. Doubt," Kerim said, stopping in front of them.

Harry could feel Serena stiffen.

"What do you want?" she said.

Kerim turned towards her and threw her a cold smile. "Just following orders Mrs. Doubt. If I were you, I'd keep my mouth shut."

Serena pushed away from Harry's arms ready to clobber Kerim with one of her Kung fu punches.

Harry pulled her back into his embrace. "Don't let him get to you."

Her body seemed to relax. "It's hard not to."

"Serena," he said. "Please try."

She gave him a quick nod of the head. "Okay, I'll *try* to behave."

Kerim smirked. "That's a good little wife."

Serena pushed Harry away and stepped towards Kerim. "Oh now, you just crossed the line, angel freak."

Kerim's men, who resembled WrestleMania goons rather than soldiers, stepped forward.

"Stand down," Kerim said, giving them the army hand signal to stop.

"Yes sir!" They stepped back.

He turned to Harry and Serena. "You both are coming with me."

Harry shot a glance at Serena. *Now what?*

From the quizzical expression on her face, she was probably thinking the same thing.

CHAPTER 26
HONEYMOON IS OVER

The wailing of the siren resonated over the campus signalling the 8 pm curfew. The wedding was officially over.

The people who had been celebrating just moments ago were now filing into separate lines, dragging their feet towards their assigned shelters located in the south side of campus where the dormitories and the sport center gymnasiums were.

It was bizarre to witness the stark contrast of the celebration moments earlier to what was unfolding before them now—masses of people moving together like docile cattle heading towards the slaughterhouse.

Kerim's voice broke his thoughts. "Escort the newlyweds to their honeymoon suite," he told his guards.

"Yes sir!" they said in unison. They moved in front of Harry and Serena, motioning with their rifles towards the East of campus. "Let's go!"

"What? No cutting of the cake or throwing of the bouquet?" Serena said. "Kerim, what kind of cheap wedding is this?"

Harry snickered. He had to admire her for having the balls to stand up to Kerim.

"Lionheart's orders," Kerim said.

Lionheart's orders? He wasn't sure what that meant, but he wasn't going to waste time thinking about it. Harry grabbed Serena's hand. "Let's go."

✦❈✦

WHEN KERIM AND HIS GUARDS ESCORTED THEM INTO THE lobby of the GN Hospital's Emergency Room, Harry had the sinking feeling that they weren't heading to the honeymoon suite any time soon.

"Where are you taking us?" he asked.

Kerim was walking ahead of them while he and Serena were sandwiched by the soldiers beside them.

Serena leaned towards him and said in a low voice, "Ready whenever you give the green light."

He shook his head and blinked his eyes once. It was the Truth Seekers' signal to wait until further notice.

"Stop here," Kerim said before heading to the triage desk.

Serena turned to one of the soldiers. "What is going on?"

The soldier was non-responsive; his jaw locked, his eyes forward, his physical movements were jerky as if he were doing break dance moves. If in fact GN successfully were deploying robot soldiers, this guy must have been one of the first prototypes.

The emergency room was filled with patients, with a group of GN security guards a few feet away from them possibly their

138

escorts. Harry noticed a young girl tug at her mother's arm and point at Harry and Serena.

Dressed in his tuxedo and Serena in her princess dress, they must have looked like they just walked off the red carpet at the Emmy's.

The little girl lifted her hand and waved before burying her face into her mother's arm. The mother glanced up and gave them a weak smile, then turned her gaze downward into her lap.

Harry could see the little girl peeking from behind her mother's arm. He waved back and flashed a smile.

"Harry, Serena!" Kerim waved for them to come over.

The robot soldier snapped his head towards them. "Let's go," he said in a monotone voice.

The four of them walked over to the triage desk where a young pretty blonde nurse was waiting.

She gave Kerim a polite smile. "I think my staff can take it from here. Could you and your boys wait in the lobby?"

Kerim returned the smile. "Sure thing, Jenna. We'll be right here waiting."

Harry had about enough of this. "Will someone tell us what the hell we're doing here?"

The nurse stood up and handed him a clipboard.

"We'll need both of you to sign authorization forms for the *Radio Frequency* ID chip implant surgery."

Serena tightened her fingers around Harry's. "What if we refuse?"

Jenna pointed to the print out on the clipboard.

"Global Nation has enforced a national medical and ID device registry required for all citizens to have an implantable device to be used to help track and ration goods and services across the nation."

"What is this?" he asked.

"That's language from the Homeland Security Act that was passed five days after the earthquake."

Serena interrupted. "Nurse, can you explain it in plain English for those of us who don't understand political legalese?"

"GN has made it mandatory for everyone to have the RF chips implants. Without an RFID chip implant, you won't be able to access shelters, services and supplies. It's not going to hurt if that's what you're worried about," the nurse said. "Oh and please call me Jenna."

"What happens to those who refuse the implant?" he asked.

"Well, they haven't implemented it yet, but I have heard rumors that GN will begin imprisoning those who refuse." She stared straight into his eyes.

"We bumped into a group of people outside of campus who said they weren't implanted."

"Like I said, it's just a rumor for now. But since you and Serena have had a lavish wedding sponsored by GN, I doubt you both can walk out of here without the surgery."

Before Harry could respond, the door to the ER ward swung open. A young Asian woman in purple scrubs came out.

His jaw dropped open when their eyes met.

Joanna?

CHAPTER 27
MEGIDDO, ISRAEL

The heat from the Middle Eastern afternoon sun scorched everything it touched. Cristal stood on the balcony overlooking the neighborhood. The dust-filled air aggravated her lungs, poked at her eyes with stinging persistence, and stitched itself into the grain of her clothes. At around noon, the heat waves danced in horizontal lines making the houses in the distance look like they were swaying, melting in the heat.

Inside Walid's home, however, an unexplainable but welcomed phenomenon was occurring—a soothing cool breeze swept through the house, an enchanted swarm of fireflies dancing around them. Walid's sisters called it their holy *misgan* (the Israeli word for air conditioner).

Cristal enjoyed the quiet moments with Walid's family. The past two days since she returned to Megiddo, she and Walid were busy connecting to the Truth Seeker satellite interranet network. With their smart phones and Walid's computer, they were able to access what was left of the Internet via their anonymous proxy servers, which cloaked their IP addresses and identity. The only websites they could access were GN sites throughout the world.

"Do you know that GN is giving free Internet for Israeli citizens?" Walid said.

"So why can't we get access without going through Harry's satellite interranet?" she asked.

"Arab sectors won't get access till after things 'settle down'." Walid shrugged his shoulders and gave her a smirk. "Which probably means never."

The business of the day never stopped Cristal from thinking about Gabriel and the others. *Did Raffe find Gabriel? Was he safe? Would she see him again?*

Sleep did not bring comfort as images of Gabriel, Kerim and Raffe haunted her dreams. Waking up in a cold sweat and greeted by the dull glow of the alarm clock's LED numbers saying that it was *3:00 am* was aggravating to say the least. Her nightmare filled nights went unnoticed by Walid's sisters who slept like hibernating bears, their gentle breathing filling the room, interrupted by the occasional grunt.

Walid and Samy had left for Tel Aviv before breakfast.

"Take me with you," Cristal had said.

"It is not safe," he replied. He always spoke to her in English, proud that he was able to. "The soldiers have checkpoints throughout Israel. The government is unstable and communication is down. Remember, you are not an Israeli citizen and they do not treat the foreigners nice. I promised Kerim to protect you and I will keep my promise."

What could she say? She was in no hurry to leave the peace of this home and family.

So Cristal entertained herself by spending time with his sisters, hoping that the world could wait to be saved for one day.

She observed the two older ones, Shaima and Nazreen, cook the afternoon meal as their mother prepared the dessert.

Wanting to show Walid's mother her talents in the kitchen, Cristal volunteered to make the rice, but regretted it soon after when the result was less than desirable—dry uncooked shrunken grains.

"I don't understand. I make rice all the time back home and it always turns out fine," she grumbled to herself.

"Not to worry," Walid's mother said. "Rice comes in many variations. Like people, one must learn how to work with them and understand their needs and differences. For instance, the rice we eat is Basmati. It is not like the Asian rice of China or Japan which is sticky and sweet. Basmati rice *tshrub miy ekteer* –drinks lots of water. Watch." She proceeded to pour a cup of water into the pot, turned the burner heat to low, fluffed the rice with the wooden spoon and finally covered the pot.

"Oh, you can add water *after* the rice is cooked?" Cristal said.

"*Akeed*! Of course," Walid's mother said shocked that she had to ask. "Lesh la? *Why not?*"

Yeah, why not? Cristal asked herself. Just because she learned how to do something one way didn't mean it had be the steadfast rule.

Walid's mother wiped her hands on her apron. "I'm going to pick the vegetables to make *salata*, salad." She opened the bottom cabinet and brought out the large oval orange plastic tub.

"Would you like me to help?" Cristal asked.

Walid's mother frowned and waved her other hand to dismiss her as she walked by her to the door. "No, no. You are a guest. You stay inside. Too hot outside," she said. She disappeared down the stairs, humming to herself a tune Cristal heard her hum every day. The tune had a soft mournful lilt that seemed to weave a melancholy tale. When Cristal asked what the song was, the response Walid's mother gave her was simply a curt "It's Om Kalthom," her tone sounding more like "how could you not know that?"

Cristal glanced out the window to see Walid's mother crouched by the vegetable patch, picking the ripest tomatoes and cucumbers and placing them into her plastic tub.

Walid's sisters had told her that the garden was a "miracle from God". Prior to the earthquake it had been an arid plot of dirt, devoid of any plant life. Strangely after the quake, vegetable plants began flourishing, the soil turning a rich black color despite the lack of water or fertilizer.

Walid was wary of the "miracle" and warned his mother that the vegetables may not be safe to eat. His mother had replied sharply, "Never question God's will."

Other so-called "miracles" were happening in different Arab sectors, Walid's cousins and friends told him while he was on his adventures outside of Megiddo.

"Are you okay, Mizz Cristal?" Nazreen asked her.

Cristal realized she'd been standing and daydreaming instead of attending to her own chores. Looking down, she saw the sink was full of dirty pots and pans, which, as Walid's mother would say, weren't going to wash themselves. She flipped up the faucet handle filling the sink with water, squeezed liquid soap onto the dishes and reached for the sponge.

Nazreen came up beside her, grabbed the sponge from her hand. "No, no. Sit, sit."

Shaima, the older sister, scooped soup into bowls and slipped the empty pot into the soapy water.

"It's okay. I can wash," Cristal said in broken Arabic. "You cook, I wash. That's the agreement, *masbuth*? Right?"

Nazreen gave her a grin and nodded. "*Masbuth!* You're right." She handed the sponge back to her.

Nosayba, the little one, burst into peals of giggles.

Shaima scrunched up her chubby face, shook her head and wagged her finger at them. "*Had msh mneeeh.* Not nice. Cristal is our guest."

"*Octee*, sister. As Mother always tells us, we mustn't argue with the guest." Nazreen grabbed her little sister by the hand, glanced over her shoulder with a devilish grin and hurried out of the kitchen.

Cristal chuckled to herself. *Who wouldn't want to be excused from dishwashing duty?*

Shaima moved beside her. "I wash. You sit." She gave Cristal a playful hip-chuck and pushed her out of the way.

"Okay, okay. You win," Cristal said, turning around. It was so nice to feel like she was part of the family.

She was startled to see Walid standing in the archway of the kitchen. "You're back already?" she asked.

"Mizz Cristal. You might want to see this." He motioned for her to join him in the sitting room.

"What is it?" She followed him wondering if something happened to Harry and Serena.

Walid's eyes darted towards the corner of the room. Cristal shifted her gaze in the same direction. A cold chill ran up her spine. She sucked in her breath when she recognized the tall dark haired man who stepped out from the shadows.

"Cristal, nice to see you again."

"Wouldn't say the same for you, Dr. Saeed," she said in a quiet voice, shooting an angry glance at Walid.

"I had no choice, Mizz Cristal," he said. "The IDF are outside holding my mother."

The pounding of her heart was crushing her ribs. *Keep calm. Think.*

Dr. Saeed stepped towards her, his snake oil salesman smile pasted on his lips.

"You don't need to be afraid," he said. "We're here to bring you to GN."

"I don't want to go anywhere with you." Waves of energy pulsed through her veins. She clenched her fists, ready to send him flying.

"Mizz Cristal, no!" Walid cried out.

Screams rang out from behind her. She turned to see an IDF soldier. It wasn't the yellow glow in his eyes that raised her hackles. It was the automatic weapon that he was pressing into Shaima's back. Her eyes were wide with fright, tears streaking down her face.

Cristal felt the room begin to spin. *Did demons take over the IDF?* She had to calm down fast and not let her powers get out of control.

Her body shook as she tried to suppress the volcanic energy erupting from her core.

"Breathe, Cristal," Dr. Saeed said in a commanding tone. "You don't want to start another earthquake and kill more innocent people."

Before she could respond, an icy blast of wind swept through the room, knocking photos from the walls and toppling Walid's mother's precious collection of crystal figurines from the bookshelf. The coldness whirled around her in circles.

Did Dr. Saeed send one of his invisible demons to capture her?

Cristal tried to calm herself by taking deep breaths but the intense vibrations shook every cell in her body. The stone walls of the house were contracting in and out.

I need to calm down.

A translucent shape appeared in front of her and vanished while the house shook violently around her and Shaima's shrill screams pierced her eardrums.

Despite all the commotion, Dr. Saeed appeared unfazed, crossing his arms and glancing at his watch.

Cristal shut her eyes. *God, I could use some help here.*

Suddenly there was a high-pitched sound, which caused everyone to double over.

The deafening wail was followed by a blast of white light that illuminated the room. Everyone froze where they stood.

And then there was silence.

CHAPTER 28
GN NEW YORK

H arry was still getting over Joanna's new look. Her long straight hair was pulled back in a high ponytail; her face was makeup free, and the nurse scrubs hung oddly on her as if they were two sizes too big.

Not wanting to blow Joanna's cover, Harry focused his attention back on the nurse.

"What if we don't comply?" he asked.

The nurse's smile quickly evaporated. She looked past him over his shoulder to where Kerim was standing in the waiting area. "Let's talk inside. We don't have much time. Joanna can lead you to the room."

Joanna nodded and pushed open the door for them.

They followed Joanna into the ER ward with the nurse a few steps behind them.

Harry and Serena sat in a small operating room waiting for the nurse to give them the run down. Joanna was playing watch guard by the door keeping an eye out for Kerim.

"Joanna and I went to school together and kept in contact over the years. We reconnected right before the quake," the nurse said.

"What does that have to do with anything?" Serena interrupted.

"I owe you my life, Harry," the nurse said, her gaze never leaving his.

"How?" he asked.

"Joanna brought me to your bomb shelter when the earthquake happened."

Harry glanced over at Joanna who looked like a cat who swallowed a bird.

"Joanna, you willfully disobeyed orders," Harry said.

"I couldn't just leave her out there to die," Joanna said, her eyes darting over to Jenna.

Ten days ago, the old Harry would have flipped out. Breaking orders meant disciplinary action or, in this particular case, cause for involuntary discharge from the Truth Seekers.

"It is a serious violation but considering the circumstances," he said with a shrug.

Serena shot him a disapproving glare.

He switched his attention back to the nurse. "So Jenna, I'm guessing you're not really a nurse," he said.

"I did study nursing for six months before I..." she began.

"... dropped out," Joanna added.

Jenna threw her a dirty look.

"Okay, so what's the plan?" Serena asked.

Jenna said, "We're going to tape a magnetic RFID tag to the bottom of your foot."

Serena narrowed her eyes. "Sorry, still don't understand how that's going to help us."

"Me neither," Harry said. He glanced around the room. He had the underlying feeling that they were being watched.

Harry grabbed Serena by the hand. "We're out of here."

"Copy that," Serena said.

They both jumped up from their seats and rushed towards the door.

Joanna waved her arms motioning for them to stop. "The tape is a decoy. I've created a program that mirrors the data that GN expects to see on your RFID. What's important is that you can control what info they see." She flipped her right shoe off, yanked down her sock and lifted the heel of her foot.

"See," she said pointing at the inside of the bottom of her foot.

"Not sure what you're trying to show us here," he said.

Joanna peeled off a tiny transparent circular piece of tape the size of a dime and showed it to him.

"Both of you are going to have to put yours on now. Kerim is outside monitoring all of this. He's going to wonder what's taking so long and if he suspects anything, we're all dead."

She turned to Jenna and said, "Give them to me."

Jenna opened a small vial where she extracted two circular transparent adhesive bandages.

"Why do we need to put the decoy tape on our feet?" Serena asked.

Joanna handed one to each of them. "It's just a precaution. If you go through a security search, it's the least likely place they'd check. But technically, you can put the RFID decoy tape anywhere on your body. When you pass the body scanners, it will send data to the security network as if you had the RFID chip implanted."

"How is this any different than having an RFID chip implant-ed?" Harry asked.

"Well, that's where my brilliant work comes in to play. We're going to show you the person tracker software I helped design for GN."

THE SOFTWARE WAS FAIRLY SOPHISTICATED ALTHOUGH THE CSS definitely had Joanna's signature all over it with hot pink headers and button icons.

Serena mumbled under her breath. "So what's this called? RFID Bubble Gum Wrapper?"

The corner of Joanna's lip curled. "Very funny" she said to Serena before turning to Harry. "This is a copy of the GN Tracker, which Lionheart asked me to program. Except I've added extra functionality."

Serena's mouth opened as if to say something. Harry put his hand on her knee and squeezed it gently signaling to her to play along.

"Okay, guys," he said. "Show us what we need to know."

They watched a computer monitor as Jenna pointed the mouse arrow to an icon on the desktop, clicked and opened the screen to a map of New York. Small green blinking icons were clumped together around major cities. The largest clump was in the location of GN University.

"Zoom in right here," Harry said, pointing to the location of the GN hospital.

"Sure thing." Jenna clicked the magnifying glass icon.

The map zoomed into the ER and then to the operating

room. Four green icons were blinking. When the mouse hovered over the icons, a popup box appeared.

Beside Joanna's avatar read *Joanna Chan, GN IT Systems Manager*.

Jenna turned to Harry. "This is a mirror of what GN Security sees. If you hover over the photo, the bio info comes up and other data such as vitals."

"Vitals?" Serena asked. "Why would GN want to know about someone's vitals?"

Joanna moved away from the door and came to join them. "Not sure why exactly. When I was in the meetings with Beaver and Lionheart, they always asked me to leave the room when the programming regarding the Vital Stats came up," she said.

Jenna clicked on a button and a new tab opened zoomed in on the four green blinking dots. She clicked on the dot that represented Joanna and dragged it outside of the room and down the hallway.

"Watch this," Jenna said. "Security thinks Joanna went to the washroom." She switched back to the GN Security view.

She clicked on the camera icon besides Joanna's blinking green dot. A new window popped up with a live stream video of the lady's washroom from Joanna's point of view.

Harry glanced over at Serena.

"So, the RFID is broadcasting what the person is seeing?"

Joanna piped in. "Yeah, pretty much. It was my idea. Clever, huh?"

"What an idiot," Serena said under her breath.

Harry squeezed her knee again.

Serena flashed him an "obedient" smile, leaned over and kissed him on the cheek. In his ear she whispered, "You're going to pay big time on our honeymoon, my dear husband."

He felt his cheeks flush red as she leaned back into her seat. How exactly was he going to be paying her back? He gulped.

Joanna put her hands on her hips and made a face. "You two want to book a hotel room? You know, Kerim and his friends will be here any minute."

Harry took in a deep breath. *It's like being in high school all over again. Can't seem to control my hormones. Focus. Think disgusting thoughts to make it stop.* Harry pictured Dr. Saeed devouring a dead lab rat. *Okay, seems to be working.*

"Continue the debriefing," he said in a commanding tone, hoping to deflect the attention away from him.

"Jenna, drag my icon back into the operating room area before anyone notices," Joanna said.

"Sure thing."

When Joanna's green icon was dragged back into the location of the operating room, the live video stream showed Harry and Serena sitting side by side and each holding a cotton pad between their thumb and forefinger of their right hands. Oddly, their hands were stained a dark orange yellow color.

"What is this?" Serena asked. "How come the video is capturing us doing something we aren't actually doing?"

The old Joanna that Harry knew began puffing up her proverbial feathers like a peacock.

"That's the added functionality I was talking about. I programmed our copy of the program to produce a 3D real time photographic model. The beauty of this is the program is so intelligent that it creates a storyline by mathematically calculating what GN Security is expecting to see. Or what we want them to see."

Serena looked at Harry with a raised eyebrow. He must have been smiling from ear to ear.

"So, your program is broadcasting what we want GN to see? The 3D modeling looks so real. I have to say that this is the most brilliant software I've ever seen."

Joanna clapped her hands with glee as she ran towards him and gave him a hug. "I knew you'd like it Harry! I told you that my degree in gaming design and 3D modeling could be put to good use, huh?"

Serena stepped forward and pulled Joanna backwards. "Hands off."

Joanna whirled around. "Or what?"

Serena spotted an office chair off to the right. She swept her foot kicking the office chair towards Joanna, and then lunged forward, grabbed Joanna by the arm and spun her around, pushing her down into the chair.

Harry gave a smirk. "Guess that answers your question." He glanced at his wife and their eyes locked for a brief moment.

Serena turned towards Jenna whose mouth was open in surprise. "Do you have anything you want to say to me too?"

Jenna was noticeably shaken. "Oh actually, forgot to say congratulations for tying the knot, right Joanna?"

"Yeah, *gong she*," Joanna mumbled in Cantonese under her breath. *Gong she* meant *congratulations* but her tone was far from sincere. Her friend gave her a stern look.

Joanna coughed. "I mean, congrats. You two deserve each other."

Jenna approached them and gave Harry two new satellite phones from the backup stash he kept in his bomb shelter.

"Joanna installed the software in both devices. But only use the 3D virtual animation when you really need to," she said. "If you're not careful, you could tip off GN security. Keep in mind that they're watching everything and everyone. Everything is being recorded. If they smell anything fishy, they'll retrieve the footage and scan for discrepancies. Lionheart has an insatiable appetite for wanting to know everything going on at GN."

Joanna added. "We can text but you'll need to use your thumbprint to prove your identity. Kerim knows our call signs and Lionheart has him by the nuts."

Serena asked, "What was the orange stuff that was on our hands in the video?"

"Iodine. It's used to disinfect the area before the surgical procedure. Why?" Jenna answered.

Serena lifted her wrist to show them that the orange beaded bracelet was vibrating and glowing a bright yellow.

"Something you should be telling us?" Harry asked her.

"We don't have much time. We have to put the iodine on our hands now. Kerim is coming," she said.

Jenna's eyes widened as she glanced towards the door. "How do you know that?"

Serena looked over at Harry and then back at Jenna. "Let's just say that my demon radar said so."

CHAPTER 29
GHOSTS

Cristal stumbled into the now all too familiar vacuum of black space. As soon as she took a step forward a giant almost life sized snow globe appeared in her path.

"Holy crap. Scared the *bejesus* out of me," she muttered to herself.

Her curiosity overcame her initial scare when she noticed that inside the globe was Walid's sitting room. She walked around and marveled at how she was able to see into the room from every angle.

Standing in the middle of the room was a doll size version of her, light softly spilling around her body. *I look so freaky.*

A miniature version of Dr. Saeed was posed exactly as she'd remembered, with his arms crossed, his eyes on his watch. On the other side of the room, stood "mini" Shaima, her face contorted in fear, her mouth open in a silent scream as the soldier shoved the barrel of his semi-automatic rifle into her back. Across from her, Walid's arms were in the air waving for "mini-Cristal" to stop before she exploded into a nuclear power plant.

In the corner of the globe, she noticed a movement, a flicker of blue light. It raced into the room, swirling and dancing as it knocked over the photos on the wall.

Inside the sitting room, the blue light circled around and then stopped in front of the Cristal inside the scene. Cristal pressed her face closer to the globe as the blue light started taking shape.

She watched in amazement as the blue light morphed into the shape of a young man. The details became more vivid; thick dark eyebrows, a slightly crooked nose but it was the dreadlocks that gave him away.

Gabriel!

And then the most unexpected thing happened. Gabriel turned and looked up right at her.

Is he looking at me?

"Cristal?"

"You can see me?"

"Yeah, I can, but it's so weird. You're standing in front of me down here and at the same time, you're a giant above looking in."

"It's weird for me too."

Gabriel scratched his head. "How did you get up there?"

She shrugged. "Beats me. I was down there one minute and here the next. The most important thing is I found you. Where've you been?"

He waved his arms and spun in a half circle. "Here, I've been here the whole time with you. Except you couldn't see me."

She recalled the cool breeze that would sweep through the house. "That was you? You were the cold wind that cooled Walid's house?"

"Yeah, that was me," he grinned. "I tried to talk to you but you couldn't hear me."

"Raffe said he was going to find you. He made it seem that you were headed down to the fiery pit."

Gabriel's face grew dark when he heard Raffe's name. "I don't trust that guy. Didn't he try to kill you?"

"Yeah, but he says that his orders have changed. He's my guardian for now."

"Guardian? Seriously? Doesn't change the fact that he still wants to catch me and drag me to Purgatory. Not sure how much time I can stay here as a ghost," he said.

Cristal's stomach flipped over. "Don't say ghost. You're not a ghost."

He gave her a sad smile. "I *am* a ghost and I've accepted that."

What could she say? She couldn't and didn't want to accept it.

Gabriel cleared his throat. "I've gone back to my apartment to look for Harry and Serena but they weren't there."

"You mean, you can travel back to New York?" She was relieved that the topic had changed.

"Yeah, but I can only stay there for two days at the most. Something keeps pulling me back here. Did you know that I've met others like me?"

"Other ghosts?"

"Yep. In New York and here in Megiddo."

"And..."

"It seems I know more about what's going on than they do." He bowed his head and grinned. "I'm kind of like their leader right now."

She cracked a smile. "You're a born leader, Gabriel. I'm not surprised."

He tapped his head and laughed. "I almost forgot! We can communicate through your bracelet," he said.

"Really? Great. How do we do that?"

"You have to focus on the rectangle charm. I'll focus on communicating to you just like how your dad contacted you."

"Sure, let's try now."

She lifted her arm and touched the rectangle charm on her bracelet, focusing her energy toward it. A jolt of energy leaped from her chest and streaked down her arm to the bracelet.

"It's working," she said.

The charms vibrated against her skin, jangling together like tiny Christmas bells. Her finger traced the edges of the rectangle charm, which was glowing a pale blue light. The rectangle peeled off and floated up in front of her expanding into a 24-inch wide screen. The blue glow melted into white noise until Gabriel's face filled the screen.

"I see you," she said.

He gave her a huge smile. "Awesome."

A far off thunderous rumbling sound caught her attention.

"Did you hear that?" she asked.

She turned back but Gabriel was gone. The globe had completely vanished, taking with it the light and leaving her standing in complete utter blackness.

Her bracelet was lifeless again, hanging on her wrist like an ornament.

"I wish I could figure out how to teleport out of here," she mumbled to herself.

"It takes some practice," a deep voice said.

She turned her head towards the sound.

"Kerim?"

The voice deepened. "Yes, my love."

Something wasn't right. Kerim had never ever called her "my love."

She whirled around. "Who are you? Show yourself now!"

"Tsk. Tsk. You need not yell," the voice said.

A blur of energy moved in front of her before materializing into human form.

CHAPTER 30
GEOENGINEERING IN GARDEN OF EDEN

The dark wide face and popcorn teeth were what greeted her. "Raffe."

"At your service," he said, bowing deeply like Mr. Bean before the Queen Mum herself. She half expected Raffe to add satire to the moment by curtsying.

"Very funny," she said. *Stay calm.*

Raffe straightened up, his cheeky smile still peeking from behind his poker face.

"I saw myself inside a globe like I was looking at a flashback of what happened before I ended up here. What was that?" She was careful to omit the part about seeing Gabriel, though chances were he had watched the whole thing.

Raffe waved his hand. "You mean this?"

Hundreds of snow globes appeared around them, each with scenes of different people. Gazing upwards, she noticed there were more globes filling the "sky"—a blanket of stars. It reminded her of the school visit at the Planetarium except for stars and planets, she was watching live streams of frightened people.

In one globe, desperate children huddled together, their eyes sunken and dark, their clothes torn and filthy. The adults, two men and two women were in a heated conversation.

"What am I seeing?"

"This is what's happening in USA, land of the free." Raffe snapped his fingers.

It was as if he had pressed the volume button up on the TV remote control.

"The kids need to eat," the dark haired woman said. "We can't keep going on like this."

The other woman nodded her head. "Maybe it won't be so bad to get the RFID chip implants. At least we'll have a safe place to stay, clean water and food to eat. Think about the kids."

The taller man shook his head and punched his fist into his other hand. "No. We will NOT be marked with the Sign of the Beast."

The shorter man waved his arms. "Come on. Maybe we interpreted the Book of Revelations too literally. How can we be sure that the RFID chip is the Mark of the Beast?"

"Please, Sam," the dark haired woman said, grabbing the tall man's arm. "Our kids are dying of hunger. Do you think God will punish us for trying to protect our children?"

The tall man pushed her away and covered his face. "I'll find food. I promise. Just give me one more day. Please..."

Raffe snapped his fingers and the sound disappeared.

Cristal's heart pounded hard against her chest. A tsunami of emotions rose up inside of her.

"I don't understand," she managed to say.

"There's more. Much more." Raffe snapped his fingers. Hundreds upon hundreds of globes appeared above them.

The globes were filled with scenes of destruction, disease, wars, violence, poverty, hunger, strife and suffering. In a haunting way the images were familiar to her as if she was in a CNN newsroom watching live footage of devastation and destruction from all over the world. The only difference was the men, women and children in the globes weren't from countries across the ocean a million miles away. The locations were recognizable famous landmarks in the USA—Las Vegas Boulevard, the Hollywood sign, the Space Needle, the Golden Gate Bridge, Mount Rushmore, the Statue of Liberty, Bourbon Street in New Orleans and more.

"Stop! That's enough!" She couldn't absorb any more of the heart-wrenching images.

Raffe clapped his hands. New globes replaced the previous globes. From the different nationalities of the people and the landmarks she came to the conclusion that the globes represented different nations. At first glance the majority of the globes resembled third world countries. One globe expanded fifty inches in width. Inside the globe, the scene revealed small hut-like houses. Off to the east, a group of boys with coffee colored skin were running and playing in an open field of manicured grass as green as the leaves of an evergreen forest.

"Is that in Africa?"

"Your geographical knowledge is impressive. That is Sudan," Raffe said.

"I wasn't sure because I expected to see a drier desert backdrop."

"Yes, odd to see green forests where deserts once covered the land."

She turned to him. "Is this what happened after the earth-quake? Did I cause the devastation in the US and the opposite effect in third world countries like Sudan?"

CHAPTER 31
PLAYING GOD

Raffe became silent, his expression almost thoughtful. "At first the higher ups blame you as cause for sudden bipolar activity on Earth."

"Bipolar activity? Can a planet have a bipolar disorder?"

"I know not what you refer to," he said before continuing. "Extreme changes in Earth's climate can cause shifts in weather conditions from all parts of world. The manifestations coincide with the time you set off earthquakes."

Raffe stepped back. "Get a load of this." He chuckled to himself pleased with his lame Jack Nicholson Joker impression.

With a clap of his hand a black curtain lifted from behind him, revealing a twenty-foot high globe. Inside, scientists in white lab jackets were staring up at a huge Imax theatre size screen. They were intently watching military cargo planes flying over open water and dumping huge amounts of a reddish chemical substance.

"What are they doing?" she asked.

"This is GN's solution to reverse effects of what you humans call *Climate Change*. They call this *Geoengineering* or in this specific case *Carbon Dioxide Reduction*. They're dumping over 100 tons of iron sulfate and 50 tons of iron oxide into Red Sea, which Sudan borders."

Cristal tried to play that out in her head. From her basic understanding it was similar to the principles of fertilizing soil except the concept was being used in the sea. "So is that why Sudan's deserts are now fields of green grass and forests?"

Raffe smirked, her answer amusing him. "What you're watching is illegal experiment which happened over past two years of human time. This experiment killed millions of fish life and destroyed marine habitats. And guess who the world brings in to investigate the destruction of the Almighty's creations? They bring in GN scientists! They conclude that evil 'Climate Change' is to blame.

"And then there is Solar Radiation Management (SRM) project, which GN tells humans it is for reducing amount of solar energy reaching earth. GN pump sulfate particles into atmosphere to mimic major volcanic eruptions in order to induce cooling effect. Do you know what happen instead?"

"I can only guess."

"It create horrible drought affecting South America, Asia and Africa or simply put, billions of humans. GN's pumping of sulfates into air eroded tropical rainforests preventing earth's natural processing of carbon dioxide."

Cristal nodded her head. "I remember watching this all on CNN. Why didn't anybody stop them? There are tons of activists out there. Surely they would have noticed all this."

"All of these experiments were done under pretense that GN was medicating earth from potential catastrophic events caused by the evil climate change. Do you think GN knew not what outcome of iron dumping and sulfate pumping experiments would be?"

Her eyes widened. "What do you mean?"

Raffe let out a loud belly laugh. "Ah, poor ignorant humans. Swallowing all sewage that TV pumps into your tiny heads."

"Okay, you have my attention. What exactly are you trying to say?"

"The rich and powerful control this earth, not countries or nations. World leaders are only puppets to spout out what they want humans to believe. Do you know about a New World Order?"

She raised her eyebrows. "Oh come on. You're telling me those conspiracy theories are true?"

He chuckled to himself. "You do not believe? This is how demons do things to destroy world right under your noses. Humans from first world societies like you live in boxed lives believing what is told to them. Democracy is just smokescreen for humans to believe that world they live in is actual freedom. It's a gilded cage."

She had about enough of his insults and the America-bashing. "What does this have to do with me? Why are you telling me all this? Please speak slowly. Your accent is wearing me out."

"My accent? Well, English is not my favorite language. Do you wish for me to switch to Hebrew instead? Or how about a bit of both?"

"Whatever makes you happy."

This seemed to relax him. He tilted his head and crossed his arms. "You want to know why the orders to kill you were changed? When you opened the portal, the earthquakes affected all GN experiments. Your stunt made GN demon plans backfire.

"Third world countries now feel the positive impact as you have just witnessed. First world countries now face devastation, poverty and chaos."

"You haven't answered my question. What does this have to do with me?"

He heaved a small sigh. "The Almighty has given you a mission."

"A mission?" Her stomach twisted into a knot.

"You must go to GN in Tel Aviv and infiltrate those who are running the show."

"Why me?" she asked. "Dr. Saeed knows what I can do. I opened the portal to Limbo. Wouldn't he try to make me do it again?"

Raffe threw her a smirk. "You forget. I will help you make the demon inside Dr. Saeed wish he never existed."

There was something he wasn't telling her.

"Tell me the truth. Why can't you waste the demon yourself?"

Raffe chuckled to himself. "Truth? You can't handle the truth!"

She rolled her eyes. He definitely had a thing for Jack Nicholson impressions.

"You will help me rehabilitate Dr. Saeed," Raffe continued.

"You mean brainwash," she interrupted.

"Just like a human, focusing on semantics and not the big picture." He sighed and raised his hand ready to snap his fingers. "Do you accept the mission assigned to you by Almighty God?"

Although every cell in her brain wanted to say no, she couldn't deny the challenge especially if it meant helping human kind from extinction.

"I accept," she said.

And with a snap of Raffe's fingers, Cristal found herself hurtling into the void between the spiritual and human world.

CHAPTER 32
BOY SCOUT

Harry stared at the cement wall, counting the minutes, the seconds. The fluorescent tubes above flickered and made a dull hum. The luxurious suite they'd been assigned was nothing more than a modern day prison cell. A curtain was the only thing separating the living area from the toilet and shower stall. There was a small mirror in the opposite corner, a double bed, a side table with a champagne bottle and two flutes already filled, a small chest of drawers and a flat screen TV on the wall.

He looked at the champagne glasses and smiled. *Serena must've filled them while I was in the shower.* Drinking wasn't his thing, but considering that this was a special occasion, he reached for one of the flutes.

Serena peeked from behind the shower curtain.

"You're still awake?" she said with a wicked smile.

He bolted up to a sitting position. He'd practiced turning onto his side while propping his head on his right arm several times earlier, while saying "You've kept me waiting" in the best James Bond voice he could muster.

"Um, yeah" spilled out of his lips instead.

"You're hilarious," Serena said with a gentle laugh.

She drew open the curtain and did a Marilyn Monroe pose, bending forward with her legs slightly apart.

"Like my Honeymoon outfit?" She was referring to her pearl white silk pajamas, courtesy of Lionheart and her seamstress.

"You...look...uh...hot..." His voice faltered, his words stumbling into a swirling pit of self-consciousness.

He glanced down at the space on the bed beside him while his heart was doing a rumba in his chest. It's not that this was his first time. He reasoned to himself that the rules were clear. Truth Seekers did not get romantically involved with each other. He had to admit that he was the only one who followed his rule.

"We've had a lot of champagne tonight. I mean..." he tried to say; instead he turned and grabbed both flutes. "I guess we shouldn't?"

Serena walked over and slid into the bed, her knee pressing gently into the side of his leg. Wisps of her hair brushed his face as she leaned over to place her lips on his cheek.

"Don't forget they're watching," she whispered taking one glass from his hand, toasting and clinking his drink without taking her eyes off of his. Harry followed her lead and did the same.

He still wasn't used to the fact that there was an RFID chip taped to his foot, which monitored his every move.

"Harry?" Serena's voice brought him back to the moment at hand.

He turned and was met with Serena's concerned stare. "Sorry, I'm still processing everything," he said, touching her chin.

"Ah," she said while reaching for the champagne and filling their glasses.

"I don't want us to regret anything in the morning. I could program a virtual honeymoon scene for GN and sleep on the floor." He cleared his throat.

A dark cloud passed across her face. "I see." Serena took a final gulp of her drink and put it on the side table.

He reached out brushing a stray wisp of hair from her eye.

She pulled away. Not exactly the reaction he'd expected.

"I guess one more glass won't hurt," Harry said. He chugged his drink back only to end up choking, champagne shooting out from his nose.

After the embarrassing coughing fit, he gave Serena a grin and was met with her stone cold glare.

"Why don't you go ahead and create the fantasy honeymoon game of your life? I think I'm going to turn in for the night, Zero."

She turned her back to him, pulled the sheet over herself and threw her head on the pillow. First it was flirting and now she was calling him by his alias? He shook his head reaffirming that he would never understand women.

"Serena, come on. Don't be like that." If he could have taken back the comment, he would have.

"I'm not being like anything. You've got some programming to work on. It's been a long night and I need my sleep."

He put the empty glass down barely missing the table. *Wow, no more drinks for you.*

He turned back to Serena, his gaze caressing the outline of her body under the sheet. *You are an idiot, Harry. Always have to be the Boy Scout.*

With a swift tug, Serena yanked the bed sheet off of him

letting the cold air brush against his bare skin, his silk boxers the only piece of clothing covering his body.

He swore he heard a giggle from the other side of the bed.

"Very funny," he mumbled to himself.

"Getting breezy over there?" she asked.

He leaned over and pulled the sheet back over him with the intention of turning over but instead he snuggled up to Serena until his body was pressed against hers. She shifted her hips, pushing back against him.

He whispered into her ear. "Still mad at me?"

"You're going to have to do better than that, Mr. Doubt." He noticed the playfulness in her tone.

"Well, Mrs. Doubt, why not bring your saucy lips over here so I can ensure that they pass the quality assurance check?" His lips found their way onto her ear lobe.

"Oh, not only will they pass QA, they're going to win the QA award of the year." She turned over shooting a pixie grin at him. "Serena Doubt has a certain ring to it."

She grabbed his face with both hands and pulled his lips onto hers.

CHAPTER 33
QUESTION MARKS

The wail of the curfew siren ricocheted inside the walls of the room. Harry, groggy and half asleep, tried to pry his eyelids open.

Instead, snippets of what happened the night before popped into his head: the interrogation, the wedding, the RFID decoys and...

An arm flailed into his face. "Shut that damn alarm off."

His hand reached over and patted her gently on her arm.

"It's the curfew siren," he mumbled. "Time to get up."

A small moan escaped from her lips. "Nuh-uh... you first. Just need a little more zzz's. Got such a bloody headache."

Lifting his head from his pillow was like lifting a three-hole bowling ball with his pinky. The pounding in his skull was excruciating. *It's our honeymoon after all.* He rolled over on his back. *Don't we deserve to sleep in?*

The banging in his head was accompanied by an even louder banging on the door.

Serena bolted upright. "Harry, my bracelet radar is going off again."

He stumbled out of the bed with his bare feet hitting the concrete floor with a smack, the sharp coldness under his soles snapping him wide-awake.

"Ten minutes 'till roll call!" Kerim called through the door.

"Or what?" Harry mumbled.

"Or else we're coming in there!"

Damn Kerim with his angel hearing powers.

"Kerim, if you can hear me, you can kiss my...." Serena said as she kicked off the sheet and leaped out of bed.

Harry could hear a distinct chuckle from behind the door.

"Oh, that creep!" Serena muttered.

Creep or no creep, this wasn't a game. They had to cooperate in order to embed themselves and infiltrate GN senior management.

"Serena, I'm going to get washed up. Pick out something for me to wear," he said, walking towards the bathroom area.

She stepped in front of him. "Nope, ladies first. Why don't you pick out something for me?" She giggled as she stepped in and drew the curtain shut.

"Very funny, Serena."

He gazed at Serena's outline as she turned on the water and stepped into the shower stall.

Kerim barked, "The clock is ticking, you two!"

"Yeah, we heard you the first time," Harry yelled back.

He went to the dresser to find some clothes. The top drawer contained men's underwear, shorts, t-shirts, undershirts and socks —all colored white. The drawer beside it contained much of the same except for the sport bras and female underwear.

"Honey? Do you want to wear boxers or a thong today?" he called out hoping that he sounded like a newly wed.

"Leaving that up to you Butter Bear," she called back.

"Butter bear? Seriously?"

He grinned knowing that she was enjoying the fact that she could tease him like this. From the top drawers of the dresser he pulled out undergarments for both of them and laid them on the bed. In the middle drawers he found multiple sets of grey tracksuit jackets and pants. The bottom drawer held towels and toiletries.

Prison garb was what he and Serena would have to wear for awhile.

He noticed that the tuxedo and wedding gown were on hangers on a hook behind the door. He didn't recall seeing Serena hang them up. Maybe she woke up in the middle of the night while he was passed out.

"Your turn." Serena came up from behind.

He spun around to see her wrapped in a white towel, her hair slicked back.

"Five minutes!" Another call from behind the door.

Serena looked over at the clothes that he'd laid out on the bed.

Harry tilted her chin and placed a kiss on her lips. "Thought that you'd look good in grey." He walked by her, smacking her behind.

"Hardy har har," she said.

HARRY DIDN'T KNOW WHAT TO EXPECT WHEN THEY LEFT THE

confines of their room. Kerim told them to follow him and like obedient children they did just that. No questions.

Kerim had a different pair of guards accompanying him today. They were much younger and smaller than the previous ones and much more rifle happy, digging the barrels into their backs.

"Kerim, tell your boys to back off," Serena said.

Kerim ignored the comment, walking ahead, his hand on his earpiece as he spoke to someone. "The transfer papers were authorized by Lionheart." He glanced over his shoulder, his eyes meeting Harry's briefly.

Upon entering the GN Sports Center, Kerim stopped in his tracks and turned around to his guards.

"You both are dismissed," he ordered.

Harry shot Serena a glance. *Dismissed?*

The guards' puzzled expressions mirrored theirs.

Then something strange happened. It was a subtle movement which no one but Harry seemed to notice. Kerim lifted his small pinky finger and a thin bolt of energy shot out and hit both guards in the head.

"That's an order," he said.

"Yes sir." They turned their movements becoming robotic and stiff.

Serena gave him a puzzled look.

When the guards were far from hearing distance, Kerim turned to Harry and Serena.

"Come with me."

CHAPTER 34
WARP SPEED

They followed Kerim into the Williams building where the Physics department was housed. Harry knew this building fairly well. They walked down the long corridors and down three flights of stairs to the bottom level.

"Where are you taking us?" Harry asked.

Kerim opened his mouth as if to speak but then began picking up his pace, waving to them.

"Keep up," he called.

Serena darted ahead, her insatiable curiosity kicking in.

"Come on, Harry," she said.

Intuition or fear was racing through his veins. Question marks were flying in his head. Why did Kerim order his guards to leave? Where exactly was he leading them? What if Lionheart's orders were to march them straight into the slaughterhouse?

He stopped in his tracks.

Serena had run ahead a few feet before slowing down. She

stopped to look over her shoulder. "Why are you just standing there? Come on! He's way ahead of us now."

"What if we're walking into a trap?" he asked, jogging up to her. Her silence was normal. He could see her thoughts calculating the possibilities in her head.

"You could be right," she said.

Kerim had reached the end of the hall, observing them from a distance.

"Yeah, the wedding, the tailored clothes, even our private accommodations. It doesn't look like anyone else here at GN gets this kind of VIP treatment," Serena said.

Kerim was still watching and waiting, not at all worried that he and Serena might make a break for it. Harry tried to swallow the lump that had been growing in his throat. *Don't show your fear.*

"Okay, when I give you the signal, we run for it," he said.

"Copy that."

"What's the hold up?" Kerim called out, his words echoing towards them.

Harry bent over, placed his hands on his knees. "Just catching my breath. Be right there."

Serena shrugged her shoulders. "Guess my husband isn't much of a track star."

Kerim replied, "Don't test my patience. Did you forget what I am?"

A blast of hot wind shoved Harry backward onto the ground. While he was lying flat on his back, he watched an invisible force pin Serena high up against the wall.

"Serena!" Harry leaped to his feet and scrambled towards her.

Kerim appeared out of nowhere and stepped in front of him, blocking his path.

"Let her go," Harry said in a quiet voice.

"As you wish," Kerim replied, snapping his fingers.

The tornado of energy that was holding Serena evaporated, dropping her to the ground.

"Happy now?" Kerim said, his eyes narrowing. "Don't make me remind you what I can do."

"You just blew me away with your impressive demon power," Serena said, rubbing her arms where the invisible thing had grabbed her.

Kerim chuckled. "Demon power? I forgot how small your human minds really are."

"So you're saying you're not a demon?" Harry asked.

Kerim turned and began walking down the corridor. "You guys watch too much TV."

Harry wasn't going to let him walk ahead without finding out what was going on.

"Where are you taking us? Did Lionheart order you to kill us?" he said.

Kerim spun around. "Lionheart? She can't order me to do anything."

Serena frowned. "So you've gone rogue? How about our RFID chips? She's tracking us."

"Let's just say, I've got Joanna working on fixing that problem," he said.

"Joanna?" Harry was confused. "You mean she's working with you?"

"So to speak."

Harry shook his head. "I don't get it. Why was she so afraid of you finding out?"

Kerim gave a sigh. "You still think this is a game. I'm not here to entertain you. Nor am I here to answer your questions. I'm your only ally right now. So stop wasting my time. I'm trying to save humankind from the brink of extinction."

Serena turned to him her eyes widening.

"Don't you think that's a tad dramatic?" Harry asked. "And aren't angels supposed to be protecting us?"

Kerim stood silent, his expression reflective. "It's ironic," he said after a few moments. "It's the demons that want to keep humans alive right now. For their own selfish reasons, of course."

Serena frowned, "And what do angels want?"

Kerim's eyes grew dark. "Rafael and his army have requested for God to wipe mankind from the face of the earth."

Harry could feel the hair on the back of his neck rise. *Keep calm.* "So Lionheart threw a huge wedding for us for a purpose. Obviously not from the goodness of her heart."

Kerim threw him a smirk. "She is trying to make an alliance with Israel, which is now being controlled by GN Tel Aviv. She knows that Dr. Saeed and the other demons need you to fulfill their plan. The wedding was a big show to prove to them that she has the upper hand."

"Okay," Harry said. "Why would Dr. Saeed care if I got married to Serena?"

"Married to Serena?" Kerim said, choking back a laugh. "You not only married Serena, you're married to the Lionheart demon family."

"What?"

"Well, at least that is what Lionheart and her demons think. You signed papers but didn't read the fine print. Luckily I switched the papers before you and Serena signed them."

He clapped his hands and then everything went black.

CHAPTER 35
TRAINING

The throbbing in his skull made his teeth hurt. He felt as though he was under the effects of a psychoactive drug. Where was he? Was this all in his mind?

A voice entered his head. "You don't seem to have the same stamina as your wife."

"Huh?" Harry tried to open his eyes.

"Don't worry. I'll get you back to your old self soon."

The voice sounded so familiar and yet—

"Just relax. I'm going to give you something to make you feel much better."

His energy spent, he was resolved to not fight back. The sounds of beeps and voices around him brought him to the realization that he must be in a hospital.

His ears picked up a female voice off to his right a few feet away. He strained to hear her, hoping that she'd help explain what was happening to him.

"How do you know he's on our side?" she asked.

"This is his father. He wants to help."

Father? Whose father?

Harry realized that one of the voices belonged to Joanna. And if that were the case, were they talking about his father? Was it Aaron who said he was going to inject him with something? Question being, what exactly that something was.

Focus and get up, he told himself. *You can do it.*

He could feel something cold being rubbed on his arm.

No! No! Stop!

A thought flashed in his head. The bracelet! Maybe he could teleport out of here if he concentrated.

He could hear the beeps from some sort of cardiac monitor. The beeps were firing in rapid succession mirroring the level of anxiety racing inside him.

"Doctor, his heart rate..."

"Silence, nurse. I must concentrate."

Harry felt the coldness of steel against his skin. *Oh my God. Are they cutting me open?*

He struggled to move his hands, his legs, anything to free himself.

"But doctor," the nurse interrupted. "The patient isn't completely under. His fingers are moving."

"A natural reaction. Happens all the time," the doctor said.

Oh dear God, please help me.

"Relax and open your eyes," a voice whispered in his ear. It was one he had wondered if he'd ever hear again.

"Mom?" Harry's eyes flickered open.

Expecting to see himself on an operating table with his father's hands deep inside his chest, he was stunned to find himself lying down on what looked like a yoga mat. Checking his surroundings, it looked like he was in a large gymnasium that was filled with fake high-rise buildings. He looked over to his left where a smaller version of the Brooklyn Bridge hung over a simulated river.

He tried to sit up, his head feeling like it was filled with rocks.

"Let me help."

Harry recognized the voice before he turned to see Serena's outstretched hand.

"Serena," he tried to say but his throat felt like it was lined with barbed wire.

"Take it easy," she said, grabbing his hand and pulling him up to a seated position. "You passed out when we landed here."

"What do you mean passed out?" he managed to say.

"Yeah, you know. Comatose, dead to the world, keeled over."

"Never mind." Sarcasm was the last thing he needed right then.

"Are you okay?"

He wished he could've said yes. The recent vision of his father operating on him wasn't settling well in his head. "What happened to me?"

Serena touched his cheek. "You were out for ten minutes."

"What is this place?" At first glance, it looked like a high-end jungle gym for grownups.

"Kerim said it's a parkour gym." She grinned.

"You mean like an obstacle training course?"

Serena looked at him, eyebrows raised. "Impressive."

He grinned. "Yeah I knew a few guys who were into that."

"Come on, get up," she said, nudging him to stand.

"I don't think I can. I need to recharge."

She pulled out a water bottle from her backpack, twisted the cap off and handed it to him. "Here drink this. It'll boost your energy."

He took a gulp, noticing the subtle tart taste of cranberry. "Guess this isn't just water."

"Kerim says it's an energy drink. There's a fridge full of them in the lounge."

"Kerim said so, did he?"

"Hey, just the messenger here," she said. "Come on, I'll show you around."

"Did he tell you why we're here?" What he really wanted to know was what was behind her sudden change of attitude towards Kerim.

She nodded, running ahead. "Check this out!"

He watched as she scaled the side of a replica of the Statue of Liberty monument like a professional rock climber.

When she reached the top of the statue's left shoulder, she turned to him.

"Come up!" She waved.

Not one to turn down a challenge, he yelled back, "Be there in a minute."

He ran to the base of the statue and touched the surface. It looked like the statue was made out of a combination of crushed rock and cement.

"Hurry up. It's getting drafty up here," Serena called down.

"Hold on." He looked up relieved to see the artificial hand-holds footholds bolted onto the statue.

He was no rock climber by any means, but he had done his share of indoor climbing when he was a student at GN. It wasn't pretty, but Harry managed to climb up to Serena.

"Congratulations. You made it," she said, her smile hiding her amusement.

"Okay, now what?" He gazed down at the amazing structures. He was relieved to see that between each building were giant landing pads lowering the chances of physical injury should he fall.

Serena gave him a sneaky grin. "Catch me if you can!"

A quick peck on his cheek and then she was off running to the edge of the rooftop and leaping to the one across. He let out his breath, not realizing that he had been holding it.

She turned around and waved. "Come on! Don't tell me you're chicken!"

No one called Harry Doubt chicken. He took a deep breath, psyching himself to make the big jump, when Kerim appeared beside him.

"Harry. I'm giving you a different assignment."

"Oh?" he said, puzzled but relieved.

Kerim waved to Serena. "You're doing great. The others are going to join you soon. Finish the circuit and meet us in the lounge after."

Harry shrugged. "Sorry, can't join you."

She shrugged back like it was no big deal, then turned, ran to the other side of the rooftop and jumped off.

"I don't understand what's going on," Harry said. "Why are we in a parkour gym? And what assignment are you talking about?"

Kerim snapped his fingers and before Harry could ask another question, he found himself in front of a huge control panel that faced a wall that was filled with flat screen monitors.

"Have a seat," Kerim said, turning a high back gaming chair towards him. "We don't have much time. Curfew is in a few hours and we have a lot to do."

A hundred questions were swirling in his head but he knew that now was not the time. He sat down and examined the control panel.

"I know you have a lot of questions," Kerim said, sitting in the chair beside him. "If you're wondering, I'm here on a covert mission from the Almighty."

Harry leaned back in his chair. "So are you still an angel? And if yes, what does that mean to me? I never really got into this spiritual crap."

Kerim's lip curled into a small smile. "Yes, still an angel but appearing on earth in human form."

"Angel of what exactly."

"I am the Angel of the Almighty God." Kerim fell silent.

Harry said, "Not a fallen angel? Just from my rough idea of how this works, tell me if Angels are good, fallen angels and demons are bad. Again, I don't know what the difference is between demons, fallen angels and all that."

"It's more complicated than that. It's like saying all humans are good or all humans are evil. Let's just say, demons are fallen angels who follow Satan instead of the Almighty. But there are also fallen angels who still follow the Almighty but are in his bad books because they have done something against His will. Those kind of fallen angels can find the Almighty's forgiveness if they prove themselves to be worthy of it."

Harry was slowly beginning to grasp the concept. "And where do you fit into all of this? Fallen angel or demon?"

The expression on Kerim's face went dark. "Neither. I serve the Almighty's army as an Archangel, like Rafael." He sighed, his impatience showing. "Now, we don't have any more time for your questions."

"Okay, but I still don't understand what this has to do with me?"

"It always had to do with you," Kerim said.

"What do you mean?" The angel speak was driving him nuts.

"Please for the sake of the non-practicing Jew in the room, speak using simple words."

Kerim stared at him blankly for a moment before cracking a grin. "I forgot how funny you could be sometimes."

"Me? Funny? You've definitely mistaken me for someone else," Harry said with a small smile.

Kerim leaned back, stretched his legs and put his boots on the table. "Might as well get comfortable. It's quite a long tale."

Harry leaned back too, stretching his legs forward. "Go ahead. I'm all ears," he said.

"Well, before I became an Archangel, I was sent to this earth as a Guardian of man. To get to the point, my first mission was to be *your* guardian angel."

"Woah, what?" Harry almost fell off his chair.

Kerim continued. "When you were a child, do you remember having a friend named Kerry?"

A flood of memories poured into Harry's head. *Kerry, of course!* Kerry was his only childhood friend. He was like a brother he never had. When no one would play with him at school, it didn't matter because when he got home at the end of the day, Kerry was already in his bedroom, ready to play Final Fantasy. Then one day, his father sat him down for one of his rare talks. His father had explained, in his scientific rational style of speaking, that his best friend Kerry did not exist. Even at six, Harry knew his father was wrong. He insisted that Kerry was real and he was going to do what it took to prove it.

He overheard his father tell his mother that Harry must have been having a delusional disorder.

It was at that time that Kerry stopped showing up.

"But I never really left," Kerim said softly.

Harry frowned. *What was he talking about?*

Kerim swung his legs off the table and sat forward. "Your father threatened to lock you up in an insane asylum."

Flashes of memory filled Harry's head. His father's grim face while he scolded his mother. "This kid is delusional! It's not normal for a boy to be so obsessed with an imaginary friend! He needs to be treated by professionals."

Kerim interrupted his thoughts. "That's when I had to stop letting you see me."

Harry forced himself to control the emotions welling up inside of him. He had always wondered why his friend Kerry had disappeared without a goodbye. Suddenly Cristal's voice filled his mind. *Never show your weaknesses.* She was right. This was not the time and the place to go down memory lane. He swallowed hard and focused on the here and now.

"Enough of that," he snapped. "I'm sick of you angels talking in freaking circles! Get to the point already!"

Kerim nodded. "Fine. There was a prediction that a high ranking demon would take over the world. To do this, he would trick humans into believing he is the new Savior."

"Don't demons want to kill us? Why go to all that trouble when they can just wipe us off the planet?"

"Souls are the life energy that God created. Only humans possess souls, making it an invaluable asset. Even I do not have a soul." Kerim paused, letting Harry absorb his words.

"You mean angels don't have souls? I mean, I never really thought about souls before." He took a deep breath and said, "Sorry for interrupting."

Kerim gave him a quick nod before continuing. "Yes, like I said, only humans have souls and most of them toss away the Almighty's precious gift like yesterday's trash. And for what? For stupid materialistic gains. Demons thrive on feeding human weaknesses."

"I still don't understand what the ultimate benefit for demons to obtain a human soul is?"

Kerim took a deep breath before he started to explain, speaking in a half excited and half exasperated voice. "There's a market for souls, and demons want their claws on as many as they can get. They believe if they obtain more souls than the Almighty, it would force Him to forfeit Heaven over to them."

Harry had wanted answers but all this supernatural stuff was way over his head. "Are you saying that demons treat souls like a monetary asset? Like gold?"

Kerim nodded his head. "Yes, you could say that."

Harry stood up and started pacing. "I want to know what in the world does this have to do with me. I mean, okay, so God sent you down to be my Guardian Angel and now you're talking about angels, demons and souls. Are you going to be telling me that vampires and werewolves exist too?" He shot a questioning look at Kerim. "You know, I think I've had enough of this. Take me back to Serena."

"You are no longer in charge here," Kerim said in a low voice. "Don't let me remind you again what I am capable of. I have a mission to accomplish and nothing is going to stop me from completing it. Understood?" He raised his hand.

"Okay, I get it." Harry fell back into his seat. *Control yourself.*

"You want to know why you? Watch and learn." Kerim waved his hand to the screens, the pictures changed to form one giant video. The video showed a young man on the operating table. The surgeon's back was to the screen but Harry could see that his right hand was deep inside the man's chest where a blazing white force was radiating out.

The young man turned towards them, his eyes pleading and his lips mouthing the words "Help me." The surgeon pulled his arm out of the man's chest, grasping on to the white force as if he were a magician pulling a rabbit out of a hat.

Then the eeriest thing happened. He turned towards the screen and placed the white force into his gaping mouth, swallowing the energy whole.

Harry's heart was racing a mile a minute realizing that the man on the table was himself. The other realization, which scared him even more, was the fact that the surgeon who had just swallowed the white force from his chest was none other than his father—Aaron Doub.

CHAPTER 36

SOUL SEPARATION

Harry's eyes were glued to the screen despite the fear crawling up his spine. It was like watching himself starring in a horror film that was coming to life. Too frightening to watch but too entertaining to stop.

Kerim snapped his fingers and the screens went black. He turned to Harry, his cold stare piercing into his.

"You saw this in your vision today. Right?" he said with a sharp tone.

Harry found himself nodding, but kept his mouth shut, so as not to reveal more than he had to. He had to figure out fast how to outsmart an angel. Which side was Kerim really on?

"What you saw was an actual event," Kerim said leaning back, stretching his legs forward and putting both hands behind his neck.

Here he goes again talking in circles. "Okay, explain."

Kerim's voice took on a darker tone as he continued. "You just witnessed the process of how GN demons extract souls from humans. As I mentioned, what you saw actually did take place."

Harry sat up. "But wait a minute. I saw myself on the table and the demon was my father! How can this be an actual event?"

Kerim closed his hands together. "The first time demons in Tel Aviv separated your father's soul, they didn't know that in order for the soul to live, they had to ensure that the physical body of the human was kept alive."

"Hold it. What do you mean *the first time?*" Harry's head was spinning.

Kerim gave a huge sigh, this time so loud it shook the walls of the room.

Harry clapped his hands over his ears, the sound piercing his eardrums.

"Sorry, my angelic voice is much too powerful for human ears," Kerim said in his human voice. "Angels must speak at lower wavelengths when on Earth. But as you can see, this conversation is wearing me down." He closed his eyes briefly before focusing on Harry. "Back to your question. I suppose I should bring some context to the story."

Harry held his breath, relieved to know that the truth was finally going to be told. Deep down inside he was terrified of what he was going to learn.

"The first experiments by GN demons were a catastrophic failure. The scientists had not yet realized the connection between the human host and its soul even after separation. When the host died, his or her soul died with it several days later," Kerim said.

"So when my dad died, the demon couldn't keep his soul alive inside of him." Kerim's words were like clues he had to put together.

Kerim continued. "When your father's soul resided inside the demon, his IQ transferred to the demon. The result was something equivalent to a full scale drug addiction."

"You mean, demons get high on smart people's souls?" Now that seemed so absurd.

With a raised eyebrow, Kerim continued. "The soul is a very powerful source of energy. Add to it special gifts such as a high IQ, it makes the soul even more powerful."

"Special gifts. So high IQ isn't the only gift that can make the soul powerful?" he asked.

"Good observation. The other gifts are the Seven Virtues. You know Chastity, Temperance, Charity, Diligence, Patience, Kindness and Humility."

"Guess these gifts are the opposite of the Seven Deadly Sins. Probably gifts that demons don't care much for."

Kerim eyebrows shot up. "Impressive. You are religious after all."

Harry chuckled to himself. "I'm not religious. But I did watch the movie."

Kerim shook his head and laughed. "You are funnier than you think, Harry."

"Well, never thought of myself in that way," Harry said. "But please finish the story. The anticipation is killing me."

"As you wish," Kerim said. "So to continue, when Aaron's soul died, the demon had to find another fix."

Every muscle in Harry's body shook as his mind absorbed the information. "And are you saying that I was that fix?"

Kerim nodded.

Suddenly the truth was something he wished he hadn't asked for. "Which means that I died too? I don't understand."

Pushing the chair back, Kerim got to his feet. "God declared the soul separation experiments to be an abomination. He ordered Rafael down to Earth to smite the demon and all humans involved in the process."

Kerim's words, mesmerizing as they were, only answered some of the questions lurking in his head. "But that didn't happen."

"Other angels such as me pleaded with God to see that the humans needed a second chance. In His infinite mercy, He agreed and decided to turn back time instead."

"Turn back time," Harry mumbled to himself.

Kerim said, "Yes. It was at this time when the Almighty assigned me to be your Guardian Angel."

"And God turned back time so that you and Raffe could fix history?"

"Yes, exactly. Except that demons soon realized what had happened. They seized the opportunity to use the second chance to perfect their experiments. From the scientific experiments, GN demons came to the conclusion that adult humans who had been either child prodigies themselves or who were parents of one carried a very special gene. This gene is what gives the intelligence and special talents that normal humans do not have. So GN demons did not just want any souls. They wanted extraordinary souls.

"So in changing history, GN Tel Aviv began targeting parents of child prodigies. Also learning from their past mistakes, they now understood that the secret of keeping the souls alive was to keep the human bodies physically alive."

It all was beginning to make sense now. His mother and Cristal's dad must have screwed GN demon experiments by teleporting to Limbo. And it explained how he saw his dead father alive and breathing at Haifa GN right before the earthquake.

"So my father didn't travel through time, did he? He was put into a coma just like my mother and the others," Harry said.

Kerim raised an eyebrow. "Actually your father did travel from the past to the present."

"He did?" Harry was stumped. "How?"

"Remember what I said when God turned back time? Dr. Saeed played a key role in allowing the demon to stage your father's death."

CHAPTER 37
MISSION IMPLAUSIBLE

arry tried to replay the moment he last saw his father in his mind.

"When I was in GN Haifa," Harry began, "I was shocked to see that my dead father was very much alive. He and Dr. Saeed were in a secret lab. My father was somewhat incoherent and babbling about how he remembered being on an operating table only minutes earlier and then he was waking up to find himself in the future. Dr. Saeed had acknowledged that my father had traveled through time. He even gave my dad a sedative."

"Saeed was probably prepping him for the soul separation surgery," Kerim said.

"The earthquake wasn't a coincidence?" Harry said raising his voice.

Kerim shook his head. "No coincidence. Saeed used the work you did with your father's research to help the demons."

Harry began to realize his part in all of this. "I was the one who discovered that Cristal could open the portals. But I thought the portals were only wormholes to the future."

Kerim said, "When Saeed discovered Cristal's abilities, GN demons from Haifa and Tel Aviv prepared their leader for the opening of the gates of Hell."

Harry gulped, his heart skipping a beat. "Is the demon who took my father's soul the same one as the first time around?"

Kerim gave him a cold smirk. "No. If it were, the Almighty could have sent Raffe to smite it, which would mean I wouldn't be here on this covert operation. Unfortunately, when the gates of Hell were opened, Bezel, a demon you never want to mess with, was let loose on the earth."

"And this Bezel demon swallowed my dad's soul and appointed himself the new President of Israel," Harry said, finishing Kerim's story.

"Your briefing is now complete," Kerim said, standing up. "We need to get you ready for your mission."

"One more thing," Harry interrupted. "Why did God change his mind about destroying Cristal? She still has the power to open all the portals to all spiritual worlds."

"He has His reasons. Enough questions. It's time to go."

Kerim snapped his fingers and before Harry could open his mouth to ask where, he was standing by himself on the ledge of a rooftop overlooking the parkour gym. He peered down to see hundreds of people looking up at him. He glanced over to the opposite rooftops to be met with more people standing and watching him.

"Woah," he said. "What is all this?"

Kerim's voice entered his head. "Your army."

"My what?" Harry couldn't believe what he was hearing.

"Your army," Kerim repeated, this time with his physical form materializing.

"Army to do what exactly?" Harry asked. *Not sure if I'm going to like what I'm about to hear.*

"To resist, of course." Kerim turned to him, his eyes drilling into his while his voice boomed into the gym.

"Do you accept your mission from the Almighty?"

Harry glanced down at the crowd below. A little girl, on the shoulders of a woman, was waving furiously at him. He realized that she was the girl from the hospital waiting room. Thousands waited for him to answer, their eyes anxious with anticipation.

"Of course he accepts!"

Harry looked over his left shoulder, shocked to see Serena beside him.

She stepped towards him, searching his eyes. "Kerim told me that you'd be leading us."

Harry felt his heart race and his insides shake. Being the leader of the Truth Seekers was one thing. How could he lead so many people, especially when doubts had been clouding his head every day since the earthquake? He wasn't equipped to fight spiritual beings. He barely understood what it all meant.

Kerim interrupted his thoughts. "Serena and I will be by your side every step of the way."

Serena grabbed his hand and held it tightly. "I believe in you, Harry," she said.

The fear that was haunting him suddenly took a back seat to the imminent task at hand. The old Harry Doubt, confident and determined, stepped forward to address the crowd.

"I accept God's mission!" he said in a loud voice.

Serena called out. "Harry Doubt, leader of the Truth Seekers is now the leader of the Resistance!"

The crowd erupted with loud cheers. "Resist! Resist!"

Serena turned, touching his cheeks with both hands and pulling his face towards hers. She gazed up at him, her eyes lit with a fiery passion. "I am so proud to be your wife," she said.

Her words touched him in a place deep in his heart. A place he never knew he had. Getting married was a convenient way to get Serena legally into the US. Who would have thought that it would impact both of them like this?

He cupped her face in his hands. "I am honored to be your husband," he whispered before pressing his lips onto hers.

The cheers grew louder from the people around them, but Harry closed his eyes, oblivious to it all. His focus was on Serena's sweet kiss, half hoping it could freeze time.

He reached up to caress her cheek. His fingers swiped empty air instead.

"Serena?"

"Harry?" The voice was familiar but not Serena's.

CHAPTER 38
COUNT DOWN

S erena was gone. Not exactly clear why he was here in this cramped dark space, he could only surmise that someone or something teleported him here.

He scanned the room, picking up clues about his surroundings. A solitary exposed light bulb hung from the ceiling and industrial steel shelves loaded with boxes surrounded him on both sides. He teleported to a closet?

"Glad you could join us."

He spun around, not surprised to see the stocky man with the permanent expression of impatience plastered on his face. Raffe.

"You brought me here?" he asked.

Raffe tipped his chin up to say "yes" then glanced over his shoulder. "Show him what he needs to know," he said.

The shape of a woman began materializing—first the waves of her hair, then her forehead, her eyes, her nose and then her mouth. Cristal.

"Harry!" She ran towards him, arms wide open as the rest of her body solidified.

"Cristal!"

She hugged him before stepping back. "We don't have long. We brought you here to GN Tel Aviv. The spot where we are standing is another place where the spiritual world and earth overlap. There are many of these 'safe places' scattered around Israel. Demons can't sense us when we're here."

Harry shot a look at Raffe. "Safe from angels too?"

Raffe gave him a smirk. "You need not fear me. I'm assigned as Cristal's guardian angel."

She rolled her eyes. "I don't need a guardian angel."

The sound of crowds cheering in the far distance filled his ears. Cristal and Raffe seemed to fade for a moment, daylight filling up the space.

"We don't have much time!" Raffe's voice boomed.

Cristal grabbed Harry's hand. "Focus. We need to transform ourselves."

The cheers and the light were competing with Cristal's words. He felt himself being pulled backwards.

"Curfew is in half an hour," Kerim's voice entered his head.

What was going on?

He could feel Cristal's fingers tighten around his. Raffe was saying something but the words were coming out warbled and slow.

"Raffe, help me. I can't hold him here," Cristal said.

Harry could feel himself slipping away from Cristal. Away from Raffe. Away from the closet.

His heart pounded as he tried to take a breath. Stumbling a few steps backwards, the scene changed again.

"Earth to Harry."

He glanced down to see Serena staring up at him. Her eyes were filled with concern. With a quick glance, he realized he was back on the rooftop in the parkour gym. Serena was exactly where she was standing before he teleported to the closet.

"Are you okay?" She grabbed his hand.

Harry's mouth was dry but he managed to say, "Yeah. Just a bit overwhelmed."

Kerim moved in front of him, a look of suspicion crossing his face. "You'd tell us if something was wrong. Right?"

Harry felt a sharp pain in his head. Raffe's voice filled his thoughts. "Whatever I tell or show you is considered classified material. You will not divulge this to Kerim or anyone."

Each word felt like Raffe was stabbing his brain with a steak knife. "Understand?"

The pain blinded him. He was grinding his teeth together to try to stop it.

Kerim said, "It's almost curfew. You have to dismiss everyone."

Harry nodded but in the back of his head, he thought of how bizarre it was for him to be speaking to Kerim and Serena while having another conversation with Raffe in his head. The odd thing was that they had no clue of what was happening to him.

Raffe's voice exploded this time like the sound of trumpets in his head. "Use your thoughts to answer me."

Despite the pain, Harry summoned his mind to respond. *Yes, I understand.*

And in an instant, Harry's head was clear, Raffe's voice vanishing and taking the pain with it.

"Are you okay?" Serena said. "You look a bit pale."

"I'm okay. Just a bad migraine is all," he forced himself to say.

Kerim handed him a bottle. "Drink this. It'll give you energy."

Harry took it and chugged it back. He felt every cell in his body bounce back to life. "Wow, you weren't kidding. What exactly is in that drink?"

Kerim gave him a half smile. "It's the Holy Spirit."

Serena added. "Kerim says that our souls need to be strengthened by God's Holy Spirit. It's working, isn't it?"

Harry looked down at his body and felt the energy surge through him. "Yes, it definitely is."

"We must go back. Harry, dismiss everyone. You're their leader now." Kerim directed his hand towards the people.

Harry looked down at the people. His people. "You are dismissed. We'll see each other again soon."

The crowds dispersed into lines and headed for the exits.

"That was easy," he said, turning back to Kerim and Serena.

"You guys are next," Kerim said. "But I'm going to fast track you."

Serena frowned. "Is something up?"

Kerim touched his hand to his ear. "Joanna, keep calm. They're heading to their cell now."

Keep calm? Was GN onto them?

Kerim waved his hand. "Let's go."

CHAPTER 39
SOULS AND VESSELS

Cristal stared at the empty spot where Harry had stood moments earlier. Her attempt to teleport him to GN Tel Aviv was only partially successful, proving that she had the power but lacked the control. If only she had more time to practice.

"We'll have to go without him," Raffe said.

She whirled around, surprised with his response.

"But you said that without Harry we won't be able to get Aaron's soul out of the demon."

Raffe said, "What I actually said was that because Harry is a descendant from Aaron Doub, there is a possibility that he could exorcise Aaron's soul from Bezel's vessel remotely."

"Vessel? You mean that the demon possesses the host's body?"

Raffe gave a deep sigh, his eyes looking up to the ceiling briefly. "It's complicated. Typically, yes, but in the case of the possessions with those used in the soul separation experiments, demon scientists discovered that in order to preserve the soul's full power, the demon had to swallow it."

"Swallow the soul?" Cristal said. "I don't get it."

"Humans and your tiny brains. We don't have time for me to educate you so I'm going to have to show you."

Raffe came towards her, placing the palm of his hand to her forehead.

A bright white light flashed from his hand briefly blinding her. When she was able to focus, she found herself standing in front of another huge snow globe.

Inside the globe, there was an operating room. On the table lay a young man with his face turned away. She realized that the surgeon was, in fact, Aaron Doub, and in his hand he was holding up a ball of white energy. She watched in awe as he tilted his head back, opened his mouth, and swallowed it whole.

"Comprehending now?" Raffe's voice snapped her back to the present.

It wasn't only the vision that made soul separation clear to her, somehow when Raffe touched her, the knowledge transferred from his hand and uploaded into her head.

"Yes, I understand now. The demon can't possess the host body and swallow the soul at the same time. The vessel in this case is someone completely different. I'm guessing a demon worshiper? Or some innocent bystander?"

Raffe raised his eyebrow. "No human is innocent. The demon must get permission from the vessel before he can possess it. With the amount of power Bezel carries, he has to be very careful which vessel he inhabits. His energy will destroy an ordinary human body from the inside out. In this case, he possesses a special human whose identity is hidden from angels."

"But that doesn't explain why the vessel looks exactly like Aaron Doub?"

"Not all demons are the same. The powerful ones can change

their physical appearance to simulate another human. This requires huge amounts of energy for demons to accomplish, which is why only the most powerful ones can do it."

She opened her mouth to ask another question.

"And to answer your next question...this applies to angels too," Raffe said.

Cristal could hear vibrations and screeching sounds outside the closet door.

Raffe put his finger to his mouth, signaling her to be quiet.

She could make out the sound of male voices on the other side of the door.

"We have to move Patient 66 to a safer location," Dr. Saeed ordered.

"Are you sure there's been a breach? We must inform the President," a deeper voice asked.

"No need to panic anyone just yet, General," Dr. Saeed replied.

"Dr. Saeed," the general said, "the patient cannot be moved without proper authorization."

"General, you and I are more than capable of moving the patient ourselves," Dr. Saeed said, his tone sharp.

Raffe waved his hand to Cristal, signaling her to come closer. Behind the door, the real Aaron Doub was kept in a medically induced coma, his body lying in a huge glass capsule similar to other patients they had found earlier in nearby labs.

With his other hand, he pushed the palm of his hand against the closet door. A soft glow of white light emitted from his palm creating a visual portal through the door into the next room.

Cristal could see Dr. Saeed and General Levy in front of Aaron's capsule.

"Not going to happen, Doctor."

"General Levy, must I remind you that time is of the essence here," Dr. Saeed said, his expression hardening.

The general turned away from him. "Then we must inform the President immediately." He headed towards the door.

"This is totally unnecessary!" Dr. Saeed followed after him out of the lab.

Raffe glanced over his shoulder. "Let's move Patient 66 and perform the exorcism."

He walked through stepping into the room.

Cristal followed behind, taking a step forward and bumping into the steel door.

I hate when he does that.

Her thoughts rattled in her head as she regained her focus. She reached for the doorknob and swung the door open to be met with Raffe's smug look.

"And the Almighty has pegged you as the one to save the world," he said.

"Very funny," she said, walking past him. "Okay, let's do it."

Do what exactly, she wasn't sure.

"We are going to move him to another location," Raffe said, walking beside her.

"Okay, great. Where are you going to teleport us?"

"Tele-what?"

"You know, travel through time and space." Was he going to be yanking her chain all day?

"I shall not reveal where we will be sending him lest GN captures you. The less you know the better."

Unbelievable!

"Dear God, give me strength to be patient with this angel you sent to me," she mumbled to herself.

"Better to direct your prayers for help to fulfill your mission," Raffe said with a snort.

He turned towards the capsule and lifted his arms in the air.

"Do as I do and repeat after me," he said.

Cristal lifted her arms.

"Bo nelech!" he bellowed.

"Bo nelech!" she repeated. *Bo nelech* was Hebrew for "Let's go." Seriously, was that all they had to say?

The room began to shake around them. She could feel vibrations from within her chest shoot up to her arms and out from her fingertips toward the ceiling.

White light blasted from Aaron Doub's capsule and in a split second the capsule was gone.

Raffe dropped his arms to his side and turned to her.

"You can put your arms down now," he said with a half grin.

Her arms dropped to her side.

"So the secret phrase for teleportation is 'Let's go?'" she asked.

He smirked. "Why? You expecting a litany of Latin words? You humans enjoy spewing words endlessly when one or two words can do."

She folded her arms across her chest.

"Now comes the dangerous part of the mission. We need to get close to Bezel," he said.

"You mean, *I* need to get close to Bezel," she said.

"Yes, that's true. If he senses my presence, it will ruin the mission." Raffe took a deep breath. "Exorcisms are difficult to do when far distance from subject. More difficult for you because it is your first time. You will need to be within twenty feet of him if you hope to succeed."

The vein on the left side of her temple throbbed a dull staccato beat. The tightness in her chest crushed her lungs. The moment was close at hand.

"Remember. Prayer and faith," Raffe said.

Cristal's head began spinning as waves of nausea crashed inside her stomach.

"Jesus said, '*Therefore I say unto you, whatever things you desire, when you pray, believe that you will receive them, and you shall have them*,'" he continued.

What was he babbling on about?

Raffe stepped towards her, placing his hand on her forehead.

"You must have faith in the Almighty and use the power of prayer to control yourself," he said.

"How?" she managed to choke out.

The walls began bending inward and outward as if the room was gasping for air.

"Simply pray and ask for help. Did not Abraham, Jesus and the Prophet Mohammed teach this? The Almighty sent this message to his human creations for centuries and yet you of little faith still wonder why you are lost."

Raffe's words were sinking in. Was it really that simple?

A prayer that she used to recite in Cathecism School came to her in a sudden flash.

She squeezed her eyes shut and began, "Dear God, some say that the sky is at its darkest just before the light. I pray that this is true, for all seems dark. I need your light, Lord, in every way. I pray to be filled with your light from head to toe. To bask in your glory. To know that all is right in the world, as you have planned, and as you want it to be. Help me to walk in your light, and live my life in faith and glory. In your name I pray, Amen."

She opened her eyes and found herself standing in an open space of brilliant white light. *Where am I?*

"Are you ready?" Raffe's voice was in her head.

A surge of energy surrounded her, drowning out her anxieties.

"Don't get too cozy. We have work to do," he said.

"No, not yet. Please let me stay a little bit longer," she pleaded.

"It's time."

His words sounded final.

"Will I ever come back here?"

"Of course. This is your safe place when you need to remind yourself that Heaven is real."

My safe place. She shivered at the thought of what was yet to come.

"It is time," Raffe said, his tone more urgent.

There was a mission to complete, and she was as ready as she would ever be, considering the circumstances.

"*Bo nelech.* Let's go," she said.

A *wooshing* sound rang in her ears, followed by a blast of light.

CHAPTER 40
FAITH

Cristal stumbled into the darkness of the closet, her hands grasping the metal shelves to keep steady. She glanced around, her eyes adjusting to the dim lighting.

"Not bad," Raffe said, materializing in front of her.

"Teleporting takes a bit of practice, but it's getting easier," she said. "Landing seems to be trickier than it looks."

The corners of his mouth twitched as he tried to hold back a grin. "Took me centuries to perfect."

"Thanks for the encouragement," she said. "Why are we back in the closet?"

He crossed his arms. "This space is merely a conduit for us to cross between the spiritual world and Earth. What's on the other side of the door is not necessarily the same location."

Cristal walked towards the door. "Intriguing. And I'm guessing that you know what's on the other side of the door."

He tilted his chin up and said, "Yes, and you can find out by touching the door. I'm assuming if you can travel between worlds, you have the ability to see through earthly solid matter."

Before he could finish his sentence, she reached out to touch the door. Nothing happened.

"Hm. Your presumptions are incorrect," she said.

He walked up to her and whispered into her ear. "Did you tell the door to let you see through it?"

"Ah, nope, I didn't," she replied.

He chuckled. "If someone calls you to say their computer is frozen, what's the first thing you ask them?"

"I ask them if they rebooted their computer."

"Well, then," he replied.

Point made.

She took a deep breath, touched the door and said, "Let me see through you."

Light pulsed from her hand creating a rectangle on the door's surface.

"There he is," Raffe said, stepping closer to the door.

Fuzzy shapes were moving around in the next room but it was hard to tell. It was like looking through smoked glass.

She turned to him. "I don't see anything. Am I doing something wrong?"

"Just tell the door again. Command it," he said.

Command it, she told herself. There's no way a door was going to give her attitude.

"I command you to let me see through you!"

It worked. The fog was lifting from the virtual window, like frost clearing from her car's windshield. A part of her wished she could relive those mundane moments of her old life but she brushed the thought away.

With a quick scan, she confirmed two people in the room. She recognized the General from earlier standing in front of the other person who was behind an executive desk. He was speaking in a rushed tone and waving his arms. She could not make out his words.

"So Bezel is in there?" she asked, her voice wavering.

"Yes." Raffe sounded reflective.

"Okay, I know we practiced this, but just a quick refresh. Can I recite the exorcism prayer from here?"

He stood silent, his gaze fixated with the conversation inside the room.

"Raffe? Did you hear me?"

He switched his gaze to her, raising his brow. "No. You will have to enter the room."

"I thought you said if we were within twenty feet, it should be fine." She swallowed the lump in her throat, and tried to push down the fear welling up from the pit of her stomach.

Raffe continued, his tone somber. "He has gained enormous power from swallowing the soul. It will be more difficult than I presumed."

"Should we call it off, then?" Her heart beat hard against her ribs.

He shook his head. "If we do not separate Aaron's soul from Bezel, his power will grow a million times stronger. We must complete our mission."

Something that had puzzled her before resurfaced. "Why an exorcism? Isn't that supposed to be used to get rid of a demon that possesses a human?"

Raffe shifted his gaze away from her. "Based on our theory, if we perform an exorcism, it should release Aaron's soul from Bezel's vessel."

Cristal stumbled backwards. "Theory? What do you mean theory?"

He turned to her. "I have never separated soul before. I have observed how humans and demons have done this, but never performed it myself."

"So I'm the first one to test out your theory? Is that why you aren't volunteering to do this?"

The shrillness in her voice caused him to wince.

"The Almighty assigned this mission to you. We do not have His permission to perform exorcisms ourselves."

"When you say 'we', you are referring to you and your angel crew." She clenched her fists.

"We do not have much time. Bezel is aware we moved Aaron's body."

"And what happens if I decide not to do this?"

"Don't try to defy the Almighty's orders, little girl. His wrath can be quite ferocious."

His words hung in the air.

There was nowhere for her to run and hide. Her father was in Limbo. Gabriel was stuck between worlds. And the cold hard fact that Harry, Kerim, and Serena had abandoned her was crushing her soul. She closed her eyes, feeling helpless and lost.

Dear God, help me.

As the words spilled from her mouth, a light like no other that she had ever seen appeared before her.

Raffe bowed his head and dropped to one knee. A thunder-clap seemed to come from Raffe's lips, but Cristal wasn't sure if she had imagined it.

The room was bathed with the inexplicable feeling of comfort and peace. The silence was deafening and it was then that He spoke.

Do not fear, my child. You have been called upon by our Father to complete your mission. You will not be alone.

"I will not be alone," she repeated under her breath.

The light radiated, shaking the walls of the room. She couldn't describe in words the utter brilliance or how familiar His presence was. Her humanity made it incapable for her to fully comprehend the magnitude of the moment.

I will give you strength through your trials and tribulations. Your faith in the Lord will set you free.

She trembled, tears streaking down her cheeks.

"I am Your servant," she said. But as the words left her lips, He was gone.

Raffe rose to his feet. "Are you ready now?"

She brushed the tears from her face and turned to him.

"I am ready."

CHAPTER 41
ALL THINGS IN PLAY

"You can go in," Beaver told Kerim, "she's expecting you."

Kerim entered Lionheart's office, sweeping the area with his gaze, confirming only one presence in the room.

Lionheart was standing behind her desk, facing the window, her back to him.

He cleared his throat to signal his presence, but she remained still.

"Ms. Lionheart, you sent for me?" he said.

Without moving, she said, "Your formality is amusing."

He took a deep breath. "You called me?"

"Come over here," she said, her voice soft and distant.

He went around the desk and stood beside her, keeping a few feet between them. He followed her gaze out the window, the darkness of the night blanketing the empty campus below.

"Don't you ever get tired of it all?" she asked.

He noticed the heaviness in her voice.

"Tired of what, exactly?"

She pointed out the window. "All of this."

"I'm not sure what you are trying to tell me," he said.

She turned to him, meeting his gaze, the irises of her eyes glowing a sulfuric yellow.

"Oh stop pretending. We both know what I'm talking about."

He threw her a look of indifference. "Shouldn't you close the door?"

She exposed her almost too perfect white teeth with her smile. "Oh, yes. See how forgetful I am in my old age?"

She waved her hand and the door slammed shut.

"Now we are free to be ourselves, as humans say," she said, reaching out to touch his cheek.

He tilted his head away from her hand. "Stop it or I'll have to leave."

"Oh come on, Kerim. You used to beg me not to stop." She ran her fingers through his hair.

He leaned back. "Shelley, don't test my patience."

She heaved a sigh, dropping her arm to the side. "No, I wouldn't want to do that."

Lurid shadows lurked at the perimeter of the room, poised to seize him at Lionheart's command.

She walked in front of him, her backside brushing his leg when she passed.

"Come sit with me." She flopped herself down on the couch, a sultry move that may have unraveled the staunchest of mortals.

Unfazed, Kerim slid into the opposite chair. Time in the human sense was not on their side. But playing the game was necessary.

He caught Lionheart's sneer, but she was quick to regain her composure. "Centuries of roaming this earth, scraping and clawing to make something for myself. Toiling to redeem myself just to prove that falling to Earth was worth it."

He narrowed his eyes. "Your point?"

She crossed her legs. "You didn't actually fall. To Earth, that is. Right, Kerim?"

He threw her a smug grin. "Not sure what you mean."

"We don't need to play games with each other. I trust my sources. I don't have the patience to continue this charade." She drummed her fingers on the couch, her long red nails scraping the leather.

He sat forward, not letting his gaze leave hers. "I would tread lightly here, Lionheart. I doubt you wish to unleash something you are not prepared to follow through with."

She flashed him a smile. "Oh, I am treading lightly."

He stood up. "Then I will dismiss myself."

"Wait," she said.

His nostrils flared. "For what?"

She waved her hand to the chair. "Sit down. I've got a proposition to make."

He fell into the chair, crossing his leg and throwing his arm over the back. "I'm listening."

Lionheart leaned forward, pressing her generous bosom against her arms. "Rules. Angels fall to Earth believing that they will be free from rules."

He sighed. "Where are we going with this?"

A dark cloud crossed her face. "Your little human female friend."

He clenched his jaw. "You are crossing the line, Lionheart. If I'm not fallen, as you say, then you are wading into a *soo-faw*."

She snorted back a laugh. "So you're speaking Hebrew now. You could have just said 'tempest.' But you want me to shake in my boots because *soo-faw* sounds so much stronger."

He narrowed his eyes. "Get to your point or else I'll be saying a lot more in Hebrew."

"Are you aware of the unusual activity at the US/Mexican border?" she asked.

"Activity?"

"A surge of illegals have crossed the border into California, Arizona, New Mexico and Texas within the past 120 hours."

"And this is something new?"

"They aren't coming alone."

He gave a tired sigh. "Now pray tell, who are they coming with?"

She shifted in her seat. "I thought you'd be the one to enlighten me."

His hand tightened into a fist. "Enough with the games already."

"Better then to see with your own eyes," she said.

He heaved another sigh before getting to his feet. "Fine. But this better be good."

Lionheart cracked a smile. "I take that as permission for me to take you there." She waved her arms in a giant sweeping motion and clapped her hands.

What should have followed was a thunderous sound with a flash of light and them transporting to the US/Mexican border. And yet, nothing happened.

Lionheart pressed her lips into a thin line.

He could see her thoughts racing in her head.

Without the grandeur of her first attempt, she clapped her hands again. Still nothing happened.

She fidgeted with the hem of her jacket, the silence growing more awkward by the second.

Kerim spoke in a low voice. "Is Bezel's presence on Earth weakening your powers?"

The sound of metal scraping metal erupted from her mouth. She yanked clumps of her hair from her head, holding them up like sacrificial offerings.

"If it weren't for my work, humans would have destroyed each other centuries ago. I kept the balance. I made the world a civilized place. I made sure to keep the demons at bay. And now it's all ruined because of your little bitch who opened the gates of Hell and let the Prince of Darkness out!"

He said, "Keep it together, Lionheart."

"Keep it together?" she shrieked, banging her head into her hands over and over, reminding him of the large waves at the *Marina Istanbul* that used to toss his boat against the dock while he slept.

Flashes of human memories slashed through his mind. The sound of Cristal's voice in his ear, the gentleness of her touch, and the love she freely gave him.

In human form, suppressing the memories, the blistery tornado of mortal emotions, was a constant struggle. But suppress them he must. Experiencing raw human emotion was as addictive to angels as cocaine was to humans. This was why only the mightiest of angels were chosen to take human form.

Lionheart's torment was only a mirror of his own.

"You need to calm down."

She shook her head. "I can't do this any more."

"There's a lot at stake. You have to get a hold of yourself." Kerim reached for her hand.

She raised her head, her gaze meeting his. Rivers of mascara stained her cheeks. Humanity had stolen the formidable angel she used to be.

"Kerim, will you help me?"

CHAPTER 42
NOW OR NEVER

Cristal sat in the waiting area outside President Doub's office, clutching a file folder. She glanced at her reflection in the glass doors, marvelling at the good job Raffe did to physically transform her. Staring back at her was the doppelgänger of Lori Pearl, President Doub's speechwriter, a heavyset middle-aged Chinese woman who was now tied up in the closet.

At that moment, a skinny woman in a drab green jacket and slacks stood in front of her. "Give it to me. He wants to review it before he sees you."

Roleplaying in online games was second nature for Cristal, so pretending to be President Doub's speechwriter wasn't a tough assignment. But without Lori Pearl's complete profile, she had to think fast on her feet.

Raffe, help me out here, she said in her head.

"That's Aisha, the president's secretary," he replied.

Okay, got it.

"Lori," the woman said, "the file, please. The president is waiting."

"Yes, of course, Aisha." Cristal handed her the file folder.

"You don't seem like yourself," the woman said, peering over her half-lens glasses. "The president isn't in a good mood today and he won't be happy to see you not at your best."

Cristal straightened her back, pushed her shoulders back and sat taller in her seat. "I'm fine. Just ate some bad *Lafa* at lunch," she said.

The woman scowled. "Ah! Did you eat at *Dabush*? I ate there earlier."

"No, no. *McDavid's*," Cristal said.

The woman scrunched her nose. "Ah, how many times have I warned you about that place? You need to have a stomach of steel to eat there."

Just then, the doors to the president's office swung open. General Levy marched out like an angry bull, mumbling obscenities under his breath.

He eyed Cristal before snapping at Aisha. "Talk some sense into him. There are more important things at hand than giving stupid speech ceremonies."

Aisha raised her brows and said, "General Levy, this is the president's weekly address. The people expect to hear from him."

The general bristled with fury, turned and walked out.

"Follow me," Aisha said, giving her a curt nod before entering the office.

Cristal rose from the chair and adjusted her skirt.

"Quit stalling," Raffe said, making her jump.

Quit yelling.

A blast of heat hit her in the face as she entered President Doub's office.

What was that?

Aisha was leaning over the desk pointing to an opened file folder, blocking Cristal from the president's view. She glanced over her shoulder and motioned for Cristal to come over before turning back to the president.

Gathering from Aisha's normal demeanor, Cristal realized she was the only one experiencing the sauna-like temperatures. She ran the back of her hand across her forehead, wiping the beads of sweat dripping from her brow.

"Mr. President, I recommend you ask Lori to rewrite this section before you leave for the next meeting. Otherwise you won't have time to edit the speech. The live stream is in twenty minutes."

Before she could move forward, Cristal felt a burning sensation under her feet, as if she were standing barefoot on a bed of burning coals.

Raffe's voice cut through her thoughts. *"You might experience delusions and hallucinations the closer you get to Bezel. Humans with special powers, like you, are prone to the devil's ability to manipulate."*

Thanks for not informing me during training, Cristal said with a sneer.

Clenching her teeth, she focused her energy to smother the blistering pain shooting up her leg.

It's not real. Concentrate on anything but the pain.

She tried to focus on the intricate design in the hand knotted detail of the rug on the ground.

"Something wrong, Lori?" Aisha said.

Cristal shook her head and forced a smile. "No, everything's fine."

But she was far from fine.

Dear God Almighty, help me, please.

Her body shuddered once she said the words in her head. An icy sensation followed, sweeping down to her feet and washing away the pain. She breathed a sigh of relief.

Thank you, God.

"Lori?"

Her gaze snapped up meeting Aisha's frown.

"Coming," Cristal said.

Aisha stepped to the side, giving Cristal her first full view of the president.

"Aisha told me that you ate some bad *Lafa* today," the president said.

Cristal's eyes widened. It wasn't the words that caught her off guard, it was the fact that it was spoken in a female voice.

Was this another delusion?

Raffe's voice answered, "*No delusion. Bezel is a powerful djin and can take many shapes.*"

Behind the desk should have sat Aaron Doub, but instead what Cristal saw was the last person she ever wanted to cross paths with again—special agent Yaffa Bauer, the bitch who was responsible for Gabriel's death.

"Lori?" Yaffa arched her brow.

Underneath the skin and bones lived an entity, vile and vicious, and more evil than evil itself. Reality and delusion weaved and unweaved before Cristal's eyes. One moment, Yaffa was sitting there and the next it was Aaron Doub. Cristal blinked hard and realized what Raffe couldn't see. *Yaffa was the human vessel that the devil was possessing.*

Cristal couldn't bring herself to say the devil's name. Being so physically close to its presence, the thought of saying its name suddenly made her nauseous. Logical or not, she resolved to use the names Yaffa or Aaron Doub, or whatever manifestation was before her instead.

Something creepy brushed against Cristal's arms, drawing its claw-like fingernails across her skin with nefarious intent. Poking, prodding, scratching at her, hinting of its suspicions that it knew that Cristal's façade wasn't real either.

Raffe's voice entered her head. *"Focus on the mission."*

Cristal gave Yaffa a half smile and patted her stomach. "Still queasy, Mr. President. But I'm fine. Do you need me to edit the speech?"

Yaffa tapped the desk with her forefinger. "The tone in the first section is fairly weak. Not your usual style of writing."

Cristal threw herself into character and switched gears. "If you want more buy-in from the general populous, then you need to show them your soft side. Once you've gained their trust, you can ram them with your proposed changes."

Yaffa rested her hands on the arms of the chair, stiff and motionless.

Could the devil inside Yaffa see through Cristal's guise? She held her breath as the seconds ticked.

Aisha said, "Lori, we need you to rewrite the first part."

Yaffa shoved her chair back, stood and turned to Aisha. "Get out," she snapped.

"Sir?"

A cloud crossed over Yaffa's face. "Did you hear what I said? Get the hell out of here."

Aisha's face erupted into a shade of burnt persimmon.

"Yes, sir," she said in a soft tone, her voice wavering. She rushed past Cristal with her head bowed and exited the room, closing the doors behind her.

Part one of the mission was accomplished—isolate the devil

to perform the exorcism. Cristal should have been relieved, but instead found herself gulping down the acidic taste in her mouth.

Yaffa sauntered around the desk, dragging her finger along the edge until she was face to face with Cristal. "You seem different today, Lori."

Cristal knew that if she screwed up, the entity before her would annihilate her without hesitation. Her outer appearance remained unruffled, despite the pounding of her heart.

Dear God, help me.

In that instance, a dam inside her head broke. Flashes of memory poured into her head. Aaron Doub and Lori together, arms and limbs entwined. Cristal didn't need any more clues. Lori Pearl was having an affair with the president.

Do whatever it takes, she told herself.

"Finally, we're alone," Cristal said in a sultry whisper. "You know how I hate having to pretend." She reached out and stroked Yaffa's cheek, repulsed by the spongy sensation. She fought the urge to retch up the imaginary *Lafa* sandwich she'd eaten.

Yaffa's features melded together twisting and morphing into Aaron Doub.

A smile, lurid yet inviting, crept up on his face. "Now that's my Lori," he said.

"Mr. President," she said in a seductive tone, hoping he couldn't smell her fear.

Aaron grabbed her wrist and pulled her towards him.

With her other hand she pushed gently back against his chest and wiggled away. A gesture meant to tease, and get her out of his grasp without blowing her cover.

"You've got a speech to give, Mr. President," she breathed in his ear.

"Ah, yes, the speech," he mumbled, his hand drifting down her arm, his fingers like talons scratching against her skin.

What did I get myself into? She tossed the thought, along with the other doubts, out of her mind, determined to complete the mission.

"Have a seat," she said. "I'll show you how the speech is supposed to be read." She reached over and picked up the file from the desktop.

"All work and no play makes the president not a happy fellow," President Doub said with a smirk. "But I'll go along with this. We'll have more time for you to satisfy me later."

His words made her want to gag.

It was now or never. In her mind, she called out a prayer to God as Raffe had instructed. She needed all the help He could give her.

Lord God Almighty, please give me the strength to do what I have to do.

Waves of energy churned inside her chest and vibrations rippled through her. She was confident that what was happening inside her affected her calm demeanor. Cristal directed the energy inside her to cover her from head to toe. *Dear God, please protect me from harm.*

Raffe's voice entered her head. *"Remember how I taught you. Repeat after me using the same lilt and cadence. This will hypnotize Aaron Doub's soul while bewitching Bezel into a stupor."*

Copy that. She was going to deliver the speech of her life.

"Good evening. Tonight, I say to you my people of Israel and to the world that Global Nation's efforts to restore normalcy to your lives since the devastation over these last few months has proved fruitful..."

The president nodded his head, his eyes glazing over. It

seemed that he was half listening and half undressing her with his stare.

Here it comes.

"Exorcizamus te, diabolum ab Aaron Doub tenet. Ite, et revertimini ad antiquitatem vestram corporis. In nomine omnipotentis Dei unicus."

The Latin words translated to: "We exorcise you, Aaron Doub from the devil holding you. Leave now and return to your physical body. In the name of the Almighty God, the One and Only."

Breaking out of the spell, Aaron Doub's lip curled, his eyes widening.

"Why you, Jezebel!" he cried out in a voice that wasn't a voice. It sounded more like the screeching of a freight train, screaming to a stop. Aaron's jaw dropped, his mouth gaping while a white force, a tsunami of energy, funneled its way out from the pit of his stomach into the room.

Cristal raised her arm, bracing herself from the waves, her energy force shield bending to the fury unfolding. It was then that she stopped substituting Bezel's name with Aaron or Yaffa. She had to face Bezel head on.

And what a sight it was. Aaron Doub's soul, or at least most of it, was outside of the human vessel while the tail end was still stuck between Bezel's teeth.

"You silly child," Bezel cried out, his form morphing into Yaffa. "You think you can steal what is mine?"

He grabbed onto the white energy with both hands and began yanking it back— a tug of war for Aaron Doub's soul.

Raffe's voice entered her head. *Repeat the exorcism!*

She cried out, "Exorcizamus te, diabolum ab Aaron Doub tenet..."

Before she could finish, an explosion of light blasted her back wards, slamming her against the wall, her force field absorbing the blow. The waves of energy pressed her to the wall, leaving her to only be able to watch the madness before her.

On the ceiling, a pool of shimmering light had materialized and Aaron Doub's soul was rushing upwards through it while dragging Bezel's vessel with it.

Cristal was unable to draw her gaze away from the absurd, yet horrifying, spectacle.

Yaffa's head was open wide. The white energy of Aaron Doub's soul became a hangman's rope dragging her body in the air. It was a *Cirque du Soleil* acrobatic stunt gone bad—really bad.

Bezel flailed the vessel's arms to grab hold of the soul, crying out in a language that Cristal couldn't decipher.

And then it happened.

The sound of tearing, ghastly and sickening, accompanied by a lamenting howl, filled the air as Aaron Doub's soul ripped at the seams, splitting in two.

The top part of Aaron's soul vanished into the ceiling while Yaffa, the vessel, catapulted down onto the ground with the shred of Aaron's soul still left in its mouth.

As far as Cristal was concerned, it was mission accomplished. Her part was done and she had to get out of there before the dust settled.

"Bo nelech. Let's go!" she cried, using the secret teleportation command.

She waited for the white light to whisk her back to the safety of the closet.

But the light never came.

CHAPTER 43
IS THIS THE END?

Concrete walls surrounded her in the ten by ten foot cell. Aside from the toilet in the corner of the room and the office chair Cristal was sitting on, the room was void of furniture. Wails, screams and murmurs echoed inside the walls through the vents. Her guess was she was in the basement of GN where they were holding the soul separation patients.

The minutes were turning into hours, maybe even days. Who knew how long she'd been stuck in this hole?

And there he sat, unblinking and relentless.

"Where is Aaron Doub?" he asked again.

He clenched his fist, prompting the blinding pain in her chest, knowing he could crush her heart to a pulp if he wanted to.

She grabbed her neck and gasped for air.

His hand relaxed, the pressure in her chest abating.

Beads of sweat trickled down her face. She'd given up convincing herself that this was all a delusion hours ago.

"I don't know. Don't you think I'd tell you if I did?" she said through gritted teeth.

The president's lips twitched. She realized that this thing impersonating Aaron Doub was more evil than human now.

"Answer the question. I can do this forever, but you, my dear, cannot," he said in a monotone voice.

At first, Cristal had been defiant and strong, but when her shield began deteriorating, her fortitude waned with it.

Now all she wanted was to sleep. And yet, sleep escaped her. The president made sure of that.

"I told you. I don't know where Aaron Doub is," she said and she meant it.

The president clenched his fist again.

"Ask your angel friend where he is," he said.

Cristal gasped, the pain in her chest like flames burning her lungs.

Dear God, Grant me the strength to endure this.

Sweet relief, though brief, washed over her.

"I have no angel friends," she said with the little breath she had left.

The president stood up, his expression apathetic. "You do realize I hate this as much as you."

"Why don't I believe you?" she said, her energy spent.

He came up close to her. "You are the one who opened the gates and set me free. Believe what you want, but I do not want to hurt you."

She stared into his empty eyes. "Then set me free and we'll call it even," she whispered.

His expression grew dark. "I said I don't want to hurt you. But it doesn't mean I won't if you give me no other option."

He turned his gaze away and walked out of the room, the door slamming shut behind him.

She slouched over in her chair, covering her face with her hands.

Raffe, where are you?

She slid to the ground, twisting into a ball. She pounded the floor with her fist.

What did I do to deserve this?

She pulled her knees to her chest and placed her head in her arms, her chest heaving in despair.

"Dear God, please take me away from this awful place."

Closing her eyes, she begged for sleep to come, but instead decrepit thoughts invaded her mind.

"Cristal, open your eyes," a deep voice said in the same way it used to wake her from her dreams.

Her eyes flickered open. A brilliant white light surrounded and embraced her while a sense of peace fell upon her.

"Do you know where you are?"

She turned and found Kerim standing beside her, his grey eyes shining. How she'd missed the sound of his voice and the touch of his hand.

"Kerim," she said, reaching out to hug him.

He shook his head and stepped back. "I'm not physically here."

A knot grew inside her chest. "I don't understand."

He gave her a tired smile. "I'm not supposed to be here. I'm on a covert operation on Earth."

The tidal wave of emotions brought tears to her eyes. "Am I dead?"

"No. You're in your safe place, but not for long." His body shimmered.

"I can't stay? I don't understand."

The sadness on his face mirrored how she felt.

Something caused him to look over his shoulder. When he turned back, his expression was grim.

"You have a lot more to endure. So you'll return back to where you were before. Just remember to have faith that the Almighty is with you," he said, his image fading.

"Wait! What about you? Are you with me too?" Angry tears streaked down her cheeks.

He flashed her a smile. "As the Almighty is with you, as I am. Always and forever."

She reached out but he was gone.

Dear Reader,

Thank you so much for reading my books. Reveal, book 3 of the Among Us Trilogy is the climactic finale of Harry and Cristal's adventure. If you want to know about the progress of my writing and other fun things, you can register to the Truth Seeker book club at the official Among Us Trilogy website at http://www.amongus.ca. In the meantime, we've included Chapter 1 of Reveal on the next few pages.

If you enjoyed Resist, Among Us Trilogy book 2, please take a few minutes to submit a review on GoodReads and the online store where you purchased the ebook. As a writer, your feedback helps other readers like you find my work. I appreciate each and every review.

For more information about my other books and film projects, visit my blog at http://www.anne-raevasquez.com or send me a tweet @write2film.

Till our paths cross again,
Anne-Rae Vasquez
Truth Seekers unite!

SNEAK PEEK OF REVEAL, BOOK 3 OF AMONG US TRILOGY

CHAPTER 1 - REVEAL - BOOK 3

A year passed. The instability caused by the global earthquake of 2013 brought numerous uprisings and invasions. The Ebola virus wiped out tens of thousands of people in the US, and hundreds of thousands across Europe, Asia and Australia. During this time, the international offices of Global Nation served as provisionary governments for each nation.

"Mankind has really gone mad!" Carlos said, waving his hand. "A Nobel Peace Prize for Aaron? He's gaining more followers calling him the Savior!"

Bina looked up, the images from the world of the living were playing out on the smooth water's surface of the pool. She shifted her weight on the stone ledge, her gaze going past him, across the yard to the house.

She was picturing how Harry looked, the last time they were together. She heaved a tired sigh. The moment with him was brief —too short for a mother to enjoy with her only child.

Watching his life unfold in the reflection pool was the only connection she had left with him after her multiple attempts at contacting him. Was he ignoring her and if so, why? The doubts in her mind left her feeling empty.

Carlos snorted, bringing her back from her thoughts.

"Look at how mankind is eating out of Bezel's hand! Why is God letting this happen?" He pounded his hand on his knee.

Unwilling to add to Carlos' tirade, she touched the water, changing the coordinates, the images now picking up the video feed from the GN network. Her face lit up when she saw the images of Harry with his arm around Serena.

"Shush. They're replaying Harry's wedding anniversary bash," she said.

Carlos replied, "Such good news to hear that Lionheart appointed Harry to be GN's top political advisor and Serena to be the Communications Secretary."

She nodded, knowing he was going off on another of his political mantras. She shut out his words, focusing on the images in the pool.

"...and it's just hilarious that Lionheart doesn't know that Harry is the leader of the resistance! The very movement that she is trying to destroy." His laughter filled the air, and echoed into the courtyard.

The image was now of Serena, Harry's wife, standing in front of the podium addressing the people.

Carlos wagged his finger. "GN needs to get the youth vote. I guess that's why Lionheart has poor Serena delivering GN's messages now."

Bina threw him a frown. "Hush. I want to hear what she has to say."

His eyebrows shot up as he glanced over to her.

She hunched over, focused on the speech.

"Good evening, fine citizens," Serena said, "As you may have heard, arrests are under way as we speak for those who choose to disobey the new orders. The detainees will remain in an undisclosed area until they have been rehabilitated and safe to re-enter society. Do your due diligence and stand up for America by standing in line for your microchip. It will save your life. Together we will make the United States of America, the powerful country it once was."

Carlos snorted again. "What a bunch of bull!"

Bina gave him a glare. "Hush!"

He pressed his lips together and nodded.

"...health care and food rations are determined on the basis of the data we receive via the data from the microchips. More rations will be delivered in the next scheduled mail drop day in your area."

Bina shook her head and sighed. "That's enough. I'm sick of this."

Carlos leaned forward and touched the water, the images now showing familiar streets. He knew that Bina enjoyed watching what happened in Megiddo, in the parallel world of the living.

He cleared his throat. "Aaron Doub or someone who looks exactly like him was seen in the streets of Megiddo."

Bina frowned. "Oh?"

"But Walid knows better than to let the real Aaron out on the streets, right?" he asked.

Bina fell silent. She had contacted Walid on several occasions, giving him instructions on how to keep Aaron in hiding. She made him believe that the real Aaron Doub was part of a witness protection program and that Bina was a secret agent.

He never questioned why she only appeared at his home, and for that she was grateful. It was the easiest place for her to appear to him as a living person. It was the parallel version of where she and Carlos lived, where both worlds overlapped.

Bina touched the water, this time bringing images that she knew Carlos dreaded seeing.

Cristal lay on the ground in her ten by ten foot cell, her hair serving as a pillow. Apart from not having a bed, she was treated better than others imprisoned in the bowels of GN Tel Aviv. GN guards gave her three meals a day, daily showers and a regular change of uniforms. But Bina knew that was of little comfort to Carlos.

He stood up and waved his fist. "Cristal! Can you hear me?"

His previous attempts at communicating with her were futile. And yet, he never gave up trying.

Bina got up and grabbed Carlos' hand. "At least, Bezel has given up asking her about where the real Aaron is."

He squeezed her hand, his body shaking as the sadness overcame him. "Will he ever release her?"

Bina drew him close to her, unable to answer.

He looked up to the heavens and cried out. "Raffe? You were supposed to protect her! You coward! How can you call yourself an archangel of God?"

At that moment, a cold breeze blew across the surface of the water. The waves erased the former images, replacing it with a new scene.

A man walking barefoot, dressed in red and white striped pajamas was wandering up a dusty street of small shops. He passed a young couple that turned to watch him.

Carlos muttered. "How can a grown man walk around on the streets like that in his sleeping clothes? And talking to himself, no doubt."

Bina's eyes widened. "He's not talking to himself. Look!"

She pointed at the grey shape that seemed to follow the man.

Carlos leaned forward. "Yes, yes, I see it."

Bina touched the water, the images zooming into focus. She gasped when the man turned. Despite the gauntness in his eyes and cheeks, his beak-like nose was a dead giveaway.

"It's Aaron," she said.

"Aaron? What is he doing outside wandering around alone?" Carlos cried out.

"He's not alone," she said in a quiet voice.

"What?"

"Gabriel is with him," she said.

"Why would Gabriel be with him?" He ran his hand through his hair and shook his head.

Bina turned to him, a look of confusion on her face. "Gabriel isn't the only one with him."

Carlos raised his eyebrows. "What?"

Bina shrugged her shoulders. "There is a man with a beard; he's wearing a white robe with sandals on his feet."

Carlos cut her off. "Aaron is wandering the streets with Gabriel and another ghost, identity unknown."

Bina put her hand up. "Wait a minute, I wasn't finished."

"Okay, finish," Carlos said, crossing his arms.

It was then that Bina smiled.

"There's an army of angels behind him."

ACKNOWLEDGMENTS

A very big Thank You to my wonderful beta readers! Their thoughtful critique and wonderful suggestions have made *RESIST* the best it can be.

Special recognition goes to Josefina Rosado, Ginny, Lauren Stoolfire and Ava Mallory who examined and pulled apart *RESIST* page by page, chapter by chapter. With meticulous detail, they provided me with their analysis of what needed changing, deleting and pointing out the parts that they loved. The feedback I received was what I needed to forge the story back together to be better than it could have ever been.

A thousand "thank you's" cannot express my true gratitude. So thank you dear friends multiplied by infinity!

Anne-Rae Vasquez

TRUTH SEEKERS BOOK CLUB

LIST OF CHARACTERS

Harry Doubt – 24 year old former child prodigy; Operations Manager for Global Nation by day; by night he is trying to find out why his mother and other parents of child prodigies were kidnapped by Global Nation in the Middle East. He is the programmer who designed and created "Truth Seekers", a popular online virtual reality game with over a million players. Changed his last name from "Doub" to "Doubt" after his father passed away stating that he was never really a father to him anyway; has dual Israeli and American citizenship.

Cristal Hernandez – 24 year old former child prodigy, graduated from Global Nation University with Harry Doubt at 19 years with a PhD in Computer Science, not religious but had a Catholic upbringing; book smart but doubts herself; just realized she has special powers and is learning to control them; fell in love with Kerim before finding out he was an angel; learned that God had sent Archangel Rafael to destroy her because her powers could open the portals to the spiritual worlds, Limbo, Purgatory, Heaven and Hell. This character was inspired by Josefina Rosado.

Serena Keensky – athletic, teaches self defense at Global Nation, has a black belt in several forms of martial arts including Krav Maga; is an avid Truth Seeker gamer; lived in many places around the world, the last being in the Philippines where her father is the ambassador for Russia; is a no-nonsense person. This character was inspired by Macqueline Cajandab.

Gabriel Windam – top player of the Truth Seekers online virtual reality game; loves the 70's era; loyal to Harry; was killed by accident trying to protect Kerim; doesn't realize he's dead.

Kerim Ilgaz – was hired to provide Security to GN by Harry; served in the Turkish army for four years prior to that; was revealed that he was a guardian angel; has feelings for Cristal; reported to Raffe (aka Archangel Rafael) until he fell.

Raffe (aka Archangel Rafael) – when in human form is an abrasive, tough Israeli; in angelic form is a formidable power; has a strange sense of humor; was on a mission to destroy Cristal.

Aaron Doub – Harry's father, famous GN Physicist who died right before he was able to prove the theory of time travel; was never close to his son; loved his wife Bina but always put his work ahead of his family; has Israeli and American citizenship.

Joanna Chan – IT support at Global Nation, a charitable organization. She takes her online gaming seriously. She has the most weapons and treasures in the alternate reality game called Truth

Seekers. She appears quiet and naive but her looks are deceiving. This character was inspired by Jeanne L.

Bina Schwartz – Harry's mother; Israeli wife and mother; denied her spirituality until she was kidnapped by GN demon scientists for the soul separation experiments; her soul escaped to Limbo with the soul of Carlos Hernadez, Cristal's father.

Saeed Nariman – GN Physicist and assistant to Aaron Doub; sold his soul to a demon; had been Bina and Harry's confidante and friend.

Shelley Lionheart – president of Global Nation University and charitable organization with headquarters around the world.

DOUBT BOOK 1: PLOT SUMMARY

Former child prodigies, Harry Doubt and Cristal Hernandez both earned their PhD's and went to work together for Global Nation University. Harry, a young and brilliant programmer is the son of a famous quantum physicist (Aaron) who died during an after-work dinner party. His father's theories about time travel were controversial. Aaron's business partner, Dr. Saeed, was also a famous experimental scientist. His mother, Bina, disappeared while volunteering on a peacekeeping mission in Palestine.

Harry developed *Truth Seekers*, an online virtual reality game. He began hiring all the best programmers and game players he could find. They all had a mission to find out what was behind the scenes of certain mysterious events. And with the development of the story we learn that some members of this team have some special abilities that are not completely natural.

Cristal is capable of producing earthquakes, although she is afraid of her powers and is not sure how they work or how to control them. During an emotional event, she caused a major earthquake which simultaneously hit many different cities in the world.

Kerim, hired as security by Harry and who later becomes Cristal's boyfriend, is capable of reading her mind. However, things are not as they appear.

The Truth Seekers find some portals that they believe to be entrances for wormholes for time travelling. They go to Israel to research one of those portals. But not everyone in Harry's team, such as Serena and Gabriel, know what is going on and what his motivations to plan his missions are. It turns out he wants to look for his father and mother. Mystery and intrigue cause turbulence in the relationship among the members of Harry's team. And during a persecution from the Israeli Secret Service to capture Kerim, Gabriel is shot and killed.

Harry, Cristal and Serena soon find out that Kerim had been posing as a human but really was a secret agent of God. His memories as an angel had been temporarily suppressed when he had accepted the mission explaining why Kerim, believing that he was human, had fallen in love with Cristal going against God's rule where *angels and humans are not allowed to be physically involved with each other*. Becoming completely human meant that Kerim could complete his mission on Earth undetected by GN demons. His mission from God was to infiltrate GN and prevent Cristal from opening the portals to the Spiritual worlds no matter what it took.

Dr. Saeed reveals that he is possessed by a demon and tries to overcome Cristal so that he can enter the portal. Raffe, a strange friend of Kerim, reveals he is the Archangel Rafael sent by God to destroy Cristal if Kerim can't stop her from opening the portals.

When Cristal's powers are unleashed in Akko, Israel, the site of what they thought was a wormhole; her powers inadvertently rip open a portal to Limbo. Harry steps into the portal, promising her that he will find her father and his mother and bring them back to Earth.

Archangel Rafael orders Kerim to kill Cristal. Kerim defies the orders and brings her to safety. Before Kerim flies into the heavens, he commands Walid, a resident of Megiddo, to protect Cristal. Megiddo is also known as Armageddon.

ABOUT THE AUTHOR

Anne-Rae Vasquez's latest novel Reveal book 3 of the Among Us Trilogy is an entrant in the 2018 Kindle Storyteller UK Contest; RESIST and Doubt, Books 1 and 2 of the Among Us Trilogy are Gold winner of the Readers' Favorite Book Awards. The Among Us Trilogy questions what is beyond the reality of this world and ties in different supernatural religious beliefs of God, Heaven, Purgatory and Hell, angels and demons, apocalypse, spirituality and fantasy by mixing themes from shows like Fringe and Supernatural to create an end of the world religious paranormal mystery thriller.

Her debut novel Almost a Turkish Soap Opera was adapted into a screenplay and later produced into an award winning feature film and web series and was her directorial debut. Her other works include: Gathering Dust - a collection of poems and Teach Yourself Great Web Design in a Week, published by Sams.net (a division of Macmillan Publishing).

In her parallel life, she hosts/produces Fiction Frenzy TV, a VLog channel featuring indie artists, authors, filmmakers and musicians. In addition to this, she is a freelance journalist for Blasting News (and previously Digital Journal) and an indie filmmaker.